Thanks to everyone

who helped me

Madras

Mystery of the Palm Leafs

by

Antonia Katharina Tessnow

Bibliografische Information der Deutschen Nationalbibliothek:
Die Deutsche Nationalbibliothek verzeichnet diese Publikation in
der Deutschen Nationalbibliografie; detaillierte bibliografische
Daten sind im Internet über http://dnb.dnb.de abrufbar.

TWENTYSIX – Der Self-Publishing-Verlag

Eine Kooperation zwischen der Verlagsgruppe Random House
und BoD – Books on Demand

© 2015 Antonia Katharina Tessnow

Herstellung und Verlag:
BoD – Books on Demand, Norderstedt

ISBN: 9783740733254

Übersetzung: Antonia Katharina Tessnow

for India

1

I am 28. Alexander and I are married less than a year when he wracks his motorbike and dies in the ambulance on the way to the hospital. I was in a train to southern Germany by the time the accident happened and when I arrived, my phone had no reception. This is why I only received the news the next day, while taking a walk in the nearby forest, where my mobile finds a connection for a slight moment.

It is November 9, 2003 and it is a friend who calls me. We are not very close. I hardly know him. He has read from the accident in the paper. Now he is like a ghost, an empty voice on the other side of the telephone, that just appears to bring tragedy into my life. He disappears immediately after we spoke. I never heard from him again.

The foundation, which my life was built on, completely collapsed within seconds. I can see no future anymore. All dreams, all hopes, all future plans are gone in that very moment. My life died together with my husband.

The next two years I drown myself in work. My studies are something to hold on to and allow me somehow to go on. I'm taking full time classes in college, work on weekends, take late evening courses and work to pay, additionally to my education, for my expenses.

Drowning myself fully in my busy schedule is my way to knock my feelings out. I don't want to know. I don't want to see. I don't want to feel. I just want to forget. It is fear that makes me act the way I do, that makes me run around my life, that makes me work like crazy, that drives me to completely tire myself out. Because I'm afraid to slip and fall into the bottomless darkness of my pain.

I don't know where to turn to. Some say: People should follow their dreams. The pictures in your head and mind point into the direction you are supposed to go. Living the ideas that are given to you are the sense of your existence. But: What, if there are no pictures? No visions? No ideas? What, if the future is dark and there is nothing to see and nowhere to go?

What is the sense of my life? What am I here for? Who am I? Where am I going? What am I going to be?

I keep my feelings bottled up and don't talk to anybody. It takes two full years until the shock over my husbands death loosens its grip.

It is during one of my classes, holistic psychology. The professor mentions the Palm Leaf Libraries in India. She tells us, that they hold the written scripts of all life stories of every man.

That is it! Nothing else is said. Nothing else needs to be said. But this is when I woke up from my inner sleep. What is that: A Palm Leaf Library? What would I find there? Maybe the answer to my destiny? The answer to my future? The answer to my life?

2

An intense research begins. I'm collecting all information about Palm Leaf Libraries I can possibly find. The legend truly says that all life stories are written on leafs and kept in India, but only from those people who will once go there and search for it.

The history of the libraries goes back to Rishis and the visions they had approximately 5000 years ago. A Rishi is a master of meditation. He is able to read in the 'Akasha Chronic'. The 'Akasha Chronic' holds the worlds knowledge, the worlds memory, the universal information of all times.

To read in the Akasha Chronic, the Rishis reach a state during meditation which is known as the 'Eternal Samadhi'. 'Samadhi' means enlightenment. Rishis are enlightened. They are no searchers, they know. They live in the constant consciousness of being part in a timeless universe. They are aware of the fact that their souls are living eternally, that they are incarnated in a body and that they are fulfilling a destined karma.

Many thousands of years ago, they were meant to receive visions, to write them down and to found the libraries.

As the legend goes further it says that every 800 years a copy of every written Palm Leaf is made because the leaves get old and fall apart.

The entire story is too unbelievable for me to believe. I cannot imagine this to be true. But the libraries *are there*. Might there be something real about them?

I, now, can see a bit of hope. Some light brightens the depth of my mind. Maybe the time of darkness and confusion will come to an end here. The idea of this legend being true lightens a fire inside of me.

The libraries, including all the leaves, are holy. The leaves are read out loud by a so called Nadi Reader, but not given away. That is an unwritten law. Even though, two German scientists were allowed to take their leaves home. They brought them to the University of Heidelberg where it was possible to do some research on their date and substance. The outcome verifies: The youngest Palm Leaf ever found, that describes a true life story, is 500 years of age.

3

Uncountable questions are flooding my mind. When this legend is real, when this unbelievable story is true, isn't it so, that everything was already written before I was even born? Has it always been clear that Alexander would die? Was it meant for us to meet, to live through a very own reality and to separate the way we did? If that is the case, than reality must have a much higher sense than I have ever imagined. But what is the message behind my destiny?

Life in India is rooted in the philosophy of rebirth and karma. It says, that the existence of the soul is infinite. It says, that all things in life are configured in a way that allows our mind to raise to the next higher level of consciousness. All circumstances in life, including the country we are born in, the family, the surrounding, everything, is not just a chance; it is meant to be. Everything is made exactly the way it is for the only and one reason: That our soul can widen and develop, for our understanding to expand and for us to grow spiritually. It all exists for the pure essence of experience.

That all sounds logical to me. I can understand the idea behind this philosophy. But to read books about it is one thing - to know about libraries which hold scriptures, thousands of years of age, describing destinies, is something totally different. Are the libraries the proof that we have more than one life? Are they proof that there are far more and higher levels of consciousness than we know of?

What does the worlds wisdom reveal about my life which I'm meant to live and which is such a burden from time to time? What is the sense behind my feelings which almost rip me apart once in a while? What is the essence of my experience and which level of consciousness is my soul supposed to reach?

I hardly finished asking myself all these questions when suddenly my life enfolds in such a way, that a trip to the libraries seems to be inevitable. The trip gets, in the most miraculous ways, organized all by itself. I am not doing anything to it. It almost seems that it was already planned before *I* got the chance to do it. Maybe it *was* already planned. It probably was. Long before I even knew that the libraries existed.

4

Two weeks after my research began I'm visiting the anniversary party of the Potsdamer Table in Teltow. It is an organization that collects food from supermarkets and gives it to poor people for free. A social food counter. I work there now for two years, every Saturday, ever since the branch in Teltow opened. Many people are there, some officials and even more visitors, and even though I know a lot of people around here I am only recognizing a few faces. I did not talk to anybody about my plans yet. Not even with my friends and family. No one knows that I plan to fly to Madras, South India. No one has a clue. Nobody a guess. But surrounded by all these people I get involved in a conversation with that guy I have only seen a few times. I don't even know his name. All of a sudden I have the impulse to say:

"I'm going to India."

"Oh really?", he is keeping his voice just as low as I keep mine, "I have a cousin in India. He lives … wait … somewhere in South India. In Ma … Ma …"

"You don't want to say Madras, do you?"

"Madras! Exactly! How did you know?"

"Can you talk to him for me?"

"Not necessary. He will be in Teltow, somewhen in two weeks or so. I'll introduce you. Than you can talk to him yourself."

Our conversation is over. No need to say anymore. I'm stunned. No one heard us. Everybody is busy having conversations themselves. It is loud. The noise allowed us to talk unheard.

The short conversation turns out to be the beginning of an invisible chain of circumstances leading my way, on which it seemed to be impossible to fail.

Another two weeks later. I am meeting the cousin from Madras. He picks a small coffee shop in Teltow, not knowing, that this is the place where I have seen my husband for the last time in my life. Mr. Bilson, whose first name also is Alexander, is already waiting in front as I arrive. I immediately recognize him even though I have never met him before.

He is nice and very friendly and he seems to enjoy me listening to his stories of India, that he chose thirteen years ago as his home country. He talks about his wife who is Indian and about the culture he understands very well. He draws with his words pictures and fairy tales in the air, funny stories and dramatic scenes, so colorful, that I can see them all.

His wife works as a flight attendance for an Indian airline. That is why he and his family are living close to the airport. He assures me that I will be picked up, spend a night at his house and stay safe in a resort during my visit. He will organize it all.

"This is the Indian way of treating a guest", he explains and smiles a smile so warmhearted and nice that I will never forget.

The next person I'm talking to, telling about my plans, is Sally, a friend. We are not too close, but she helped me through the long and dark nights of grief and despair, even though she never knew my husband.

I have no idea why, but just as I am telling her about the Palm Leaf Library she says:

"I owe you something. Let me take care of the ticket, will you?"

What does she mean? I have no idea. I rather feel that *I* owe *her* a lot! A lot of time, a lot of patience and an endless number of uplifting words.

A few days later I find my ticket to India in my mailbox. I'm not surprised. Right now I'm not surprised about anything anymore. I'm so into the legend of the libraries and the idea about the Rishis and their visions that nothing seems to be happening by chance anymore. Everything seems to be destined. The short conversation with the guy I hardly knew, the meeting with the man from Madras, the ticket from Sally in my mailbox, everything is happening as it is supposed to. I'm just waiting, watching. I'm an observer of my own life that enfolds right in front of my eyes.

And now there is someone else in the picture of my life. A close friend who is very important to me. We spend almost every evening together, sometimes without even really talking or doing anything. She lives two blocks away from me, not even five minutes by walk. During the day we write SMS and when she comes home from work I usually go see her. Sometimes I take a book with me and when we hang out on the couch, she watches TV, I read. Just being together feels good to us.

On a certain point of time, not long before the mystery of the leaves entered my life, we discover the 'Lord Of The Rings' trilogy and we are fascinated. The fantasy world which opens up through the story is a good distraction for our minds and our lives, which require lots of strength from each of us.

'Lord Of The Rings' tells the story of Frodo who must destroy the ring of evil, symbol of darkness and destruction, to save the world so it can be reigned by light and love. And it tells the story about his loyal, devoted friend Samwise Gamgee, called Sam. Sam is always there and supports Frodo with whatever he does. He undergoes all efforts to help him and follows him through every kind of trouble.

The character 'Sam' touches my heart. I also want to have a 'Sam', and that is exactly what I'm telling my friend. I'm longing for someone to share my life with. A companion and comrade, an ally who gives me strength and support. Because sometimes I feel so overwhelmed by my feelings that I don't know how to cope with them. Maybe someone like a 'Sam' in my life could safe me from falling? And it seems like I will fall, sooner or later, unless a miracle happens. Especially when I keep doing what I do right now: Drowning myself in work and studies, running away from myself without taking a second to breathe! Such a good friend like Sam, as described in the movies, might rescue me from my life and its heaviness. And to be rescued from my life and its depressing moments is what I long for during sleepless nights which sometimes appear to be endless.

5

November 15, 2003. My exams are up. It is my 30th birthday and I spend all day studying. My flight leaves on November 30, through Paris to Madras. I already took an exam earlier this year and passed through physiology. Now, holistic Psychology and veterinarian Science are up. The hardest and longest class, holistic medicine, will be finished somewhen during May 2004. This is what I will concentrate on as soon as I get back.

I'm excited. The last trip I took is 15 years ago. I visited Poland together with my mom. Alexander and I never went anywhere. Every moment we spend together was like being on vacation. There was no need to go somewhere.

Nothing extraordinary ever really happened. My life went relatively smooth. Only when Alexander died I sank into this endless circle of work, college and studies which kept me going and my eyes shut. It is time for this crazy lifestyle to come to an end.

My trip to India is now official. I don't keep it secret anymore. Even though I don't tell everybody, some know and the news are spreading. After my exams, before my trip, there is one more person I meet who turns out to be part in this weird chain of circumstances. His name: Alexander. He is a student in the dame college I am, going for holistic medicine, too.

"When you go to India, you HAVE to read 'The Alchemist' from Paulo Coelho! Have you ever heard about it?"

"No, I haven't. But I don't think that I have the time to go and buy a book before I leave."

"You HAVE to read this book, believe me!", he persists.

"I don't have time! I have to work and also study, ya?"

"You HAVE to read it! This book is made for you! I'm telling you!"

"I ... I ... don't know ...". Actually I wanted to say that I don't want it, but who knows why I'm meant to read this thing?

He smiles.

"Okay", I'm giving in.

"Okay! Let me get it for you", he says, "but to make it clear: If you don't read this book on your way to India, I will never talk to you again!"

"I got it!"

The bell rings and we have to go to class. Just on my last day in college he truly brings that book. I thank him and take it, then I go home and pack. The book goes into my handbag.

November 30th, four o'clock in the morning. The taxi leaves to the airport Berlin Tegel. The roads are empty. The city still sleeps. I'm wide awake.

While the plane takes off I'm staring out of the window. I immediately recognize buildings and places that are linked to all kinds of memories. I see the horse stable beside the Olympic Stadium where I work. I see the Charlottenburg Parlais and Brandenburg Gate which get smaller and smaller until they vanish from my sight.

I'm on my way to Paris. There is no direct flight from Berlin to Madras. International flights are only leaving from the big airports in Europe: Paris, Frankfurt, London.

The airport in Paris is gigantic. Thank God that I have enough time to find my way through this labyrinth of Hallways, uncountable signs and arrows. After a while I find my gate. While I sit and wait, the waiting area becomes more and more crowded. Many Indians. I can tell by their dresses, the color of their skin, the black hair and the marks on their foreheads that most of them wear.

The check-in begins. My excitement is going up.

Inside the plane are three long rows of seats. One on each window site, one in the middle. I get seated. I'm supposed to sit in the middle row in a middle seat. It is so stuffy that I wonder whose brilliant idea it was to design planes like that. Human beings do not become miraculously smaller only because one builds small seats, do they? Who is supposed to sit in here for eight hours? Me! Great! I squeeze myself into the seat, feeling like an orange squeezed into a juice.

I look around. The last row by the window is empty. The emergency seat! This is an emergency, no doubt. Right after the plane takes off we are allowed to move around. I immediately change my seat. Now I have *two* all by myself.

My adventure begins right here. I'm looking out of the window. The next stop is Madras. All I have to do is to wait.

We fly over Germany, Austria, the Alps which are stunning to look at from above. I can hardly believe it: I'm really sitting in an airplane flying into another world and I'm still the same. Will I stay the same?

6

As my feelings of awe release me, I'm taking the book Alexander has given to me: The Alchemist. I'm reading the back of it to see, what it is all about. The book talks about a boy who is dreaming about a treasure in an oriental country, and who leaves his home to find it. But instead of gold and goods he finds something 'that can never ever be taken away from him ever again'.

I open the book and start reading:

'People need not fear the unknown if they are capable of achieving what they need and want.

We are afraid of losing what we have. But this fear vanishes when we understand that our lives and the history of the world were written by the same hand', Paulo Coelho writes.

My colleague hardly knows me. We never really talked to each other. There has just been this short intermezzo where he has given this book to me. Nobody at the academy knows my history. No one knows what drives my decisions, no one knows my feelings, the desperation and the emptiness deep inside of me that drives me out of the life I have lived until this trip began.

The book talks about following signs. And that we should not get hasty or become impatient, otherwise we would fail to see the signs and omens left by God along our path. He talks about being closest to the Soul of the world when we wish for something, when we wish for something with all our heart. Because it is a positive force.

How long have I not had a true wish, captured in this futureless life?

But my trip to the libraries has been a wish, hasn't it? Didn't I desperately *want* to go there? Throughout the last weeks my life has configured itself all by itself accordingly to that wish so that I, now, sit here in this juice-squeezer, really going to India. Unbelievable!

'Actually, it wasn't that those things in themselves revealed anything at all; it was just that people, looking at what was occurring around them, could find a means of penetration of the Soul of the World', Coelho writes further.

Maybe I hope to find the meaning of the soul of the world in India? Maybe I hope to get closer to the Soul of the World? To find peace. And happiness?

I feel alone. I feel left behind. I feel weak. Going into denial took so much strength away. I didn't even look left or right once, let alone that I have realized a single sign along the way.

Further the boy meets a seer and wants to know his future. The seer described in Coelhos book says: 'I know the science of the twigs, and I know how to use them to penetrate to the place where all is written. There, I can read the past, discover what has already been forgotten, and understand the omens that are here in the present.

'When people consult me it's not that I'm reading the future; I am guessing at the future. The future belongs to God, and it is only he who reveals it, under extraordinary circumstances. How do I guess the future? Based on the omens of the present. The secret is here in the present. If you pay attention, you can improve upon it. And, if you improve on the present, what comes later will also be better. Forget about the future, and live each day according to the teachings, confident that God loves his children. Just trust. Each day, in itself, brings with it an eternity'.

'Confidence' doesn't mean much more to me than any other empty phrase. 'Trust' is a hollow word with no meaning. How can I trust? How can I be confident? What can I set my trust in to? That we're always taken care of? I have desired to die much too often, longed for death as the liberation of my pain too intensely that I feel able to look confident into live, to set trust in it, to be hopeful. I'm not able to believe in good anymore. I feel my confidence got robbed and my hope is taken away from me.

I miss Alexander to no end. It hurts so much to think about him that I'm afraid to allow this pain to fully reveal itself. This is why I'm running away. I paralyzed myself. Used all my power just to distract myself from my own grief.

I hate the world. I hate all things. I don't want time to go on. I want to hold on to it! I want it to stop! I want to turn it back to the moment when everything was all right. I can't be confident about life; I can't trust that time will tell and heal, because it is time that slowly carries me away from the last moment we have spend together.

7

Further the book talks about following the signs that are send from the depth of the universe into our personal life and to follow what the heart tells us. It talks about that our heart is where we will find out hidden treasure. This treasure must be discovered so that everything that we experience can make sense. And it talks about the sad scenario that can take place if we fail to follow the whisper of our heart and miss the possibility to find our treasure. We got to be careful not to lose ourselves within the variety of all things. Because it might happen that we forget about the search and that we put our life under the service of somebody or something we don't belong to; we unlearn how to read signs, because they don't reveal themselves anymore to us as soon as the conscience about them is overpainted by short term amusements, and than forgotten and gone. The ability to recognize the signs will fade and we'll find ourselves as slaves to all kinds of things and love-stories. Maybe one day we'll wake up and understand that we did not follow our personal path of life and that, now, it is too late, 'without that we ever understood that life and love never keeps a man from living his Personal Legend. If someone abandons that persuit it is because it was never true love … the love that speaks the language of the world'.

Has my 'love' kept me from following the way of my heart? In some ways, yes. Because my heart is broken over the loss of it and no one can follow a broken heart because it can't show any way anymore.

'Everyone on earth has a treasure that awaits him', his heart said. 'We, people's hearts, seldom say much about those treasures, because people no longer want to go in search of them. We speak of them only to children. Later, we simply let life proceed, in its own direction, towards its own fate. But, unfortunately, very few follow the path laid out for them – the path to their Personal Legends and to individual happiness. Most people see the world as a threatening place, and, because they do, the world turns out, indeed, to be a threatening place.

So we, the hearts, speak more and more softly. We never stop speaking out, but we begin to hope that our words won't be heard: We don't want people to suffer because they don't follow their hearts.'

Or don't dare to follow their hearts because they can't bear the suffering. Not to be able to cope with pain and suffering is no sin; neither it is weakness. It is life itself that sometimes puts us in front of unsolvable situations and problems, because of which many break apart or fail for none of their fault. The abyss of feelings that some look into can be so frightening that running away seems to be the only solution.

At the end of his journey, the boy finally meets an alchemist who tells him, that we never see the great treasures in the world when they are right in front of us because we don't believe in treasures anymore; and that the world is only the visible part of God. That everything is possible when we love because in such a state of mind life takes place inside of us. And most of all: That we should not give in to despair. Otherwise we can't communicate with our heart that is supposed to be our guidance on the search for our treasure.

I'm deeply touched because I'm also searching for the connection to my heart and for love that I somehow lost during all the countless, long nights of tears, loneliness and darkness. I'm searching for my treasure. The shepherd has found his. I, on the contrary, am just staying at the beginning of a search from which I only know now that it is one.

8

Because of the book two flight attendances, one after another, came up to me and started talking:

"Oh, this story is an eye-opener", the one said enthusiastically.

"It gave me so much strength and power", so the other one.

The more people are reacting to that book, the more I sense the magic it holds. And the longer I read, the deeper I fall into it. Unfortunately I'm not alone for long. A man sits down beside me, without asking, without waiting for my approval:

"Oh, you are reading the Alchemist", he almost screams. Then he immediately starts talking:

"I've been very sick. This book has brought a lot of hope to me. And the faith that everything can be good again someday. My life went into a completely new direction. When I overcame my sickness I went to the Dalai Lama in Dharmsala."

I'm listening without saying anything. I'm just nodding once in a while. This man is unsympathetic to me. He talks too loud and is very self-centered.

"I'm a banker from New York. I was the financial adviser of the Dalai Lama. I'm going to visit my parents in Chennai. This is how the Indians call Madras, did you know that?"

Even if I would have wanted to answer, I couldn't have. He is talking without the slightest brake. It almost seems he doesn't even breathe.

"I have so many friends everywhere in the world! In the United States and in India of course ..."

"Would you please leave. I would like to read", my first try to interrupt him. He doesn't.

"So many friends! Oh man. I have so many friends! I'm living in the States for 20 years now ..."

"I would like to be alone", my next try. Failed.

"My father is sick, you know? But he has a nurse at home. This is how it is in India. And my mother is there, too. He is taken care of. I don't have to worry about it ..."

"The book is exciting. I would like to keep on reading!"

"I have three brothers and two sisters. They are all living in America. My sister just got her first baby yesterday. That must have hurt! Poor thing. She lives in Atlanta. And I'm on my way to Chennai, can you believe this?"

He does not stop whatsoever. He wants to know where I come from, what I do and why I'm going to India. I don't feel like talking. Confident that he will be leaving when he gets my contacts I'm giving this strange man a business card from me. I just published two new CD's with piano music. If he is such a brilliant banker as he claims to be, and if he has only half of all the friends he says he does, maybe he buys some.

He is fine with my business card. He handles me one of his, writes another number on the back than the one that is printed on the front, gives it to me and leaves. Finally! I don't care for his card. I let it fall into my bag and keep on reading.

The man I met will turn out to be the most important person throughout the next years of my life. His name is Sam. The Sam I wished for and prayed to meet. I never imagined he would appear in the shape of an investment banker who I would unbelievably learn to love and to live with.

9

We reach Madras at 11 pm local time. Tropical heat; still-standing air and a faint smell of urine welcomes us as we get out of the plane. It smells as if the air stood here for the last hundreds of years without moving a single millimeter.

The population of Madras is approximately 7,3 million. It is the 5th largest city of India and the capital of Tamil Nadu. It was an important center of the British Empire during the 135 years Britain reigned over this country. Between 1813 and 1947 this colony was very much exploited by the British. The local industry completely collapsed, as a result of which 40 million Indians died on hunger. But the most peaceful resistance ever reported in worlds history lead India to its freedom. Under Mahatma Gandhi, on August 15, 1947, India declared its independence. The country regained its right of self governance and the world a new symbol of peace and humanity.

Every woman I see is wearing a sari. Flight attendances are wearing saris. The women at passport control are wearing saris. How unimaginable it would be to see women at a German airport wearing a feminine dress. On the opposite: No matter what kind of public place you ever enter in Germany, the women have to wear a masculine uniform. It's not gonna take much longer and the Germans will put their women in suits and ties.

Every Indian who comes out of the airport has about 1000 relatives. Each one is waiting and waving. It is crazy! Fortunately there is a fence between the mass of people and the ones just arriving. I believe this is only there so we won´t get crushed within the first seconds.

At the end of the fence I see Alexander waiting. He has something very Indian, but he still isn't Indian enough to be waving as crazy as everyone else. He just stands there. Still. The German way. But his look has something Indian. All these years of living in this country must have made him become like that. Or has he always been this way? Dark, full hair, tainted skin. He could be a native Indian though. Maybe this is reason why he chose India as his home country?

His driver takes us to his house. I cannot stop looking out of the window. It is dark. There are hardly any streetlights. But what I see outgrows all fantasies I had so far: There are people everywhere. Many people. Unbelievably skinny people who lie directly on the concrete around the sidewalks. Are they sleeping? Do they live there? Are they dead? I can not tell.

Alexanders house is indeed not far from the airport. He designed it and had people doing the construction. In India, everything is done *by* someone employed by the family, not by the family themselves: The household, the driving, the cooking and, most of the times, even raising the kids.

I'm entering a huge room. A little river flows right through the middle of it and divides the room in two. The water is meant to cool the house. The first half I'm standing in is the living room. A bridge goes to the second half which is designed to be the kitchen.

The room I spend my first night in is in the first floor. I'm sharing the children´s room together with Alexanders son and daughter. We share a bunk bad. I sleep on top, the children below and the maid right on the floor. I am very tired and fall asleep soon after I arrived.

The next morning I awake early. I'm here! I'm in India! I'm in Madras! I have to poke myself to make sure this is not a dream.

It is real. I'm not dreaming. My first day begins.

Quickly I get dressed, rush downstairs, slip into my shoes and go outside. The same heat I already felt yesterday, when I first got here, hits me again right in my face. Tropical heat. The air is filled with all kinds of tropical sounds. I can hear monkeys screaming. Until now I only knew monkeys from the zoo. Birds singing in weird voices and there are strange noises from everywhere. Sounds like the background sound of the rain forest. The one they show on TV anyway. Except that there were no cars in the documentaries I've seen so far. Here I can hear them clearly from the crowded streets a bit further away. They are giving a permanent honk concert and their far away but loud motors underline the scene.

People go past me, speaking Indian, in this part of India Tamil. I have never heard the sound of this language that is just as new as the noises around me. Dogs freely walk around and the air stands just as still as it did yesterday in the long hallways of the airport.

I get a car and a driver from my graceful host. He brings me to the hotel that is booked for me and where I'm supposed to stay.

The situation on Madras' streets makes it impossible for a German to drive. Especially when he is only used to the neat and regularized way of driving there is in that country. To drive in Madras you have to be:

1. Being born here, 2. Being be a trained driver who does nothing else than that all day long, 3. be suicidal.

The streets are totally overcrowded. I'm looking into an ocean of vehicles. Everybody drives the way he wants and everyone wants to be the fastest. Each one tries to make it into the next, little, tiny space, just millimeters away from the one in up front, the one on both sides and the one behind. Margins of safety don't exist.

There are only a few traffic lights installed by the roadside. But even though they are operating the way they are supposed to, no one really cares. They are more like a well-intended recommendation. They are definitely not there to practically establish order. Everyone drives the way he wants.

It is amazing to see how many cars fit into a single street. Between them: An uncountable number of Rickshaws. These are small, yellow, three-wheeled taxis that are open on the sides. They spread like flies over the streets of Madras. Plus: A lot of motorbikes that carry entire families. The man in front, the women in the back, carrying the children in their arms. No one wears a helmet.

But everybody hits his horn. The entire time. It is so loud that it is impossible to talk, impossible to understand a single word even when we scream at each other. The words sink somewhere into this unknown world, unheard. But people don't honk because they are aggressive. This is only what honking in Germany means. In this country it is like saying: Careful, I'm here! The problem is, that everybody who is here is making sure that the rest of mankind knows that they are here all the time.

Nonstop. Except of the cows. The only ones not honking.

In India cows are holy. A cow is understood as an aspect of God. And Gods aspects continuously niggle along the streets, lie down whenever they feel like it and take their siesta right where they are. The ocean of cars flows around them and nobody cares, nor the drivers, neither the cows. They only ruminating, lying or just standing, staring into the noisy mass before them just like a German cow stares into the nothingness of a great, empty field. I don't see any differences.

10

The name of the hotel I check in to is 'Green Madows'. Walking distance to the ocean. It is more like a little resort than an ordinary hotel. It is made out of some 15 little houses, each holding about three rooms, all in a nice park with palm trees, swimming pools and lots of my living room plants, palm trees of all kinds. Much nicer than the ones in my small apartment of course.

Although Madras' streets are loud and the noise is heard everywhere I sense a strange kind of peace. I'm not able to tell what it is caused by. It's not the kind of peace born out of stillness; but it is a deep, fundamental peace that feels very comfortable. Is it the people who carry it inside? Is it the myth of this country? The philosophy in which this land is rooted in? Or is it me? Maybe my astonishment to really being here, my excitement, my expectations?

Mr. Bilson drops me off at the hotel:

"The driver is coming tomorrow morning at eight. The car is for you. Have it for the rest of your trip. Or how do you want to get around otherwise?"

He gets into the car and is gone before I'm even able to react.

The long awaited visit to the library is planned for tomorrow. For the rest of the day I'll be all by myself. Alone. I don't like to be lonely, but I love to be alone. Right now I am happy to be just be by myself, enjoying not to feel lonely at all, even though - too often during the last long years - I have been both the same time.

I'm walking around the resort. Every Indian I see smiles. In a hotel one could expect that, but no matter if it is late at night at the sticky airport or on the loud and crowded streets, There is no difference: People see me and smile. How friendly! The Germans are very different in this matter. Many are full of bitterness. They look very unhappy. Why? I don't know. Maybe for similar reasons I am? Maybe not. I met very cold hearted and judgmental people. People who called me arrogant just by looking at me. I've been the target of such kind of judgements every once in a while. Again and again I tried to disprove, but most of the time I failed. Sometimes it's enough for me to just sit there, quietly, and people avoid me.

My way leads me to the lobby. The lobby is a relatively big area without walls or windows, but a roof. The space between the carrying elements is free. Without anything. Windows are not necessary. The climate allows the architects to built lobbies like this.

Even when it's raining season it is warmer then it is in Germany during a warm summer day. The tropical heat is comparable to a sauna running 24 hours a day, forced on everybody, no matter if they want it or not.

I go sitting on a couch, carved out of wood, covered with leather. The tea table is just as elegant but made out of stone, the top out of glass. There is no one else around but me. No other guest, nobody. I'm the only one. I turn around. The man behind the reception sees me and nods.

Half an hour later a waiter comes.

I'm ordering some water and a tea.

The Problem is that the man who takes my orders has actually a totally different job. That means, his job is to take my orders but not to take care of the tea. Forget about the water. The tea is made by the kitchen. So far so good. To bring the message from the reception to the kitchen is, again, the job of a completely different man who only does this and nothing else. The kitchen is located directly besides the lobby. Only a door separates these two. But the message-guy is, right now, unfortunately busy delivering the message of another guest's order, but he will consult the kitchen as soon as he is done.

Fine. What about the water? I'm watching the guy who first took my order and about 15 minutes to explain the hotels stuff configuration to me. Now he's having a discussion with the receptionist. The receptionist and the waiter are also two different people of course. To check in a hotel guest and to take an order are two completely different things which have to be treated as such, that means: Separately. Even though there is no one else but me in the whole wide world of this little hotel-park that also can be easily overviewed.

The receptionist is making a phone call. The waiter is smiling every time I look at him. Both are constantly shaking their heads.

It takes quite a while when another man comes out of the kitchen. He also shakes with his head but does not smile. He doesn't even see me. After approximately ten minutes he walks right through the lobby, passes me, takes the way to the entrance and goes right to the main gate. There he talks to the man who is responsible for the gate, the gate-man so to say. The gate-man is nodding and closes his gate. In the middle of the day! During the busiest time! He closes the main gate. And follows the other man to the lobby. Both pass me and disappear behind the reception. It takes maybe another 15 minutes when the gate-man opens a little door behind him, grabs a bottle of water, puts it on the desk, goes back to the entrance where he reopens the gate.

Okay, that's how it is: The gate-man is, the same time, the 'take-the-bottle-out-of-the-closet-man'. But, don't think that one of the three gentleman, who are now all standing behind the reception, takes it and brings it to me. No way! But they are all smiling. And shaking their heads.

Right, I remember: There still is the message-man. Does he even exist? And if he does, where might he be?

He exists. 20 minutes later a man comes out of the kitchen. He talks just as endless with the waiter as the gate-man did, turns around and vanishes behind the kitchen door. I have a sharp guess who that was.

I'm right. Half an hour later someone comes out of the kitchen and puts a little tray with a tea on the desk. Now it's getting really exciting!

Unbelievable! The waiter is moving! He seriously does take the tray and brings it! I am amazed! Only the water bottle he did not touch yet.

"There is still a glass missing", takes him 20 minutes to explain.

Is there a bringing-a-glass-from-the-kitchen-man? And if there is: Where is he? Hopefully not on vacation. Because it is really hot! The sauna is running relentlessly on full power and sweat is running down on me. I'm very thirsty.

It is really fascinating to see that everything, really EVRYTHING, goes in slow motion here. It took them 90 minutes to make a tea and to bring it.

The water followed 45 minutes later.

11

It's already dark when I decide to go down to the beach. The street is just plain sand, no gravel, no pavement. On the right and on the left are small shags, some made of sheet metal, some out of stone. People live there. I take a quick view inside of one as I walk by. I can see a small room without furniture where people lie on the blank floor, sleeping. The room is lighted with one light bulb from the ceiling, no lamp. I cannot see another room. That is the only one there is.

All of a sudden a vision appears in front of my inner eyes: *I'm walking through a street like this one, living in*

India. A shock-wave runs through my bones. Because I immediately feel the difference between a vacation *to* and a life *in* India. People who live here don't have a way out into another world like I do. I only have to book a flight and go back home to one of the richest countries in the world. In my vision *I don't have that option either*. For a few moments I can sense complete hopelessness. Scary!

The picture is clear and in full color. Just like someone lifts a curtain and provides a small view into my future. As if I'm meant to see this. I've no idea where this vision comes from. I only know it's there.

A few beggars are down by the beach. They are coming towards me just as they see me. These people are so poor that they force themselves on everybody without embarrassment, driven by thirst and hunger. They are of all kinds: Grown-ups, elderly, children. And they all have one thing in common: They are under weight. They are so skinny that looking at them reminds me of pictures from Nazi Germany. I remember in school they made us look at Photographs showing people in concentration camps. They looked just as thin as the ones confronting me right here. They are literally skin and bones. Starving humans. Small people, hardly teeth in their mouths and hands so weak that I wonder how they can hold a few rupees or a piece of bread.

I sit down by the water and look over the ocean. I don't know how long I'm sitting there. But I know that my entire life passes through my memory. Will the life I feel so trapped in come to an end now? Can I stop running from myself and my pain? Will my soul finally find its long awaited peace? Right now, everything I'm going through at home seems to be so far away that my memories of the life I'm living in Germany almost feels unreal. Where have I been all these years? What did I do? I don't remember a single moment of awareness. I was paralyzed and dull from my pain, crazy and tired.

I'm so tired that I would like to sit here for the next thousands of years, looking over the ocean, uninterrupted; only to recover from my sadness and to find the strength to go on.

Is there a life after death? Are we pure consciousness? Does the soul lives forever? Are we only different pieces of something greater than we are, that breathes us and keeps us alive? Are all experiences we make only steps on the way to our own enlightenment? Is there a deeper sense behind the relationships that are given to us and that touch our hearts? Are they meant to be signs? Are they here to support the development of our soul?

I can't see any sense in Alexanders death. I just can't see it. I feel alone and miss him so much that I'm blinded by my loneliness. I'm mislead into darkness and can't see no way no more.

I had goals and my life a direction. But this is long ago. This is so long ago that thinking about it almost feels like remembering a past life. What do I believe in? I don't know anymore.

What is life all about? What is the reason for us being here? Is there one?

The next day begins early in the morning. I hardly slept. But no jet-lag can be greater than my excitement which keeps me wide awake. In a few hours the long way from Teltow to Madras will reach its final destination.

Eight o'clock in the morning. I'm waiting for the driver. It is nine when he arrives. I get into the car. The driver knows where we are going. Again we are driving through the chaos of this major city, side by side with other vehicles, stop and go almost the entire way. It is loud. It is sticky. And everyone is somehow circling around the cows.

All I know about the library is that they need a fingerprint to identify my leaf; assuming the legend is true.

The ride takes an hour when we finally get there. I'm getting out of the car to find myself in front of a two story building: The Palm Leaf Library. The house looks pretty ordinary. Some of the light green tiles under the one and only balcony are partly gone. The facade looks old. It is warm. It is hot. And the air is full of peace.

There is a little waiting area in front of the entrance. Simple, wooden planks are installed for people to sit. And directly on the wall is a sign painted in green color on white ground: 'Thumb impressions will be registered between 8.30 am and 9 am'. A smile rushes through my face.

It's just past ten. Early morning in India and I'm early, too, no matter what the sign says. Traffic lights, time, numbers, all just vague ideas somewhere up in the air. No one is around yet who speaks English. The people who work here are speaking Tamil and some a little Hindi.

Both languages which don't make it any easier for me to communicate. But people here know what has to be done.

A man comes out and takes me into a small room on the ground floor. It is decorated with an altar, symbols and figures of Gods, flowers, fruits. Incense are burning. Indian music is playing.

The man indicates me to press my thump first on an ink pad and then on a piece of paper. As we're done he takes me up to the second floor, to a room where I'm supposed to wait.

There are about 25 chairs, all in lines, facing one direction. Looks like a movie theater; or one of my classes in college. The only difference is that there is no professor who talks about anatomy. Instead there is a TV showing Bollywood.

There are maybe seven people in here. All of them turn around as soon as I enter the room. They stare at me as if I was a being from another planet. And maybe that is exactly what I am in their eyes. What they see is a white skinned woman with blond, long hair, blue eyes and compared to them relatively tall. The contrast to these dark skinned, black haired, brown eyed, short people couldn't be more incisive.

I'm smiling. They're all smiling back, each one of them. Their eyes stick on me like glue sticks to a piece of paper. But right now I would rather like to be alone and sink into the all-embracing stillness which is around and which is so wonderful. It carries a shade of relief within that I long for right now.

A lot of things in this country are unexplainable to me. Bollywood is definitely one of them.

The Indians take rebirth and karma for absolutely granted. They are so used to mysticism and true legends that it is totally normal to watch TV while waiting for entire life stories written on leafs, thousands of years old. And here, Bollywood is *the* trend. Bollywood is, compared to real life, bright, colorful, happy. These stories provide a good contrast to the mostly sad reality of the streets which are full of poverty and despair.

Every year the Indian film industry produces more than America and makes more profit than Hollywood, of which most people think it is the biggest and most successful movie producing place in the world. But it is not. Bollywood is huge. Bollywood shows happy stories from a happy world. Indians *love* Bollywood.

I'm going down to the first floor to sit outside on the balcony I saw when I arrived. Nobody is here. I'm alone. I can see the houses on the other side of the road and the sandy street in front of the library.

There are hardly any vehicles. There are hardly people. It's a very quiet part of Chennai. Every ten minutes or so a rickshaw drives by, no cars. Cats and Dogs stray around and cows are everywhere. Every one strolls through the streets and each one of them with the same inner peace. And all of them in slow motion.

An hour has passed by the time the translator arrives. Someone comes and takes me to a small room with no air-condition and just a small, slow running fan. November is the hottest time of the year. Temperatures are up in the 100th. The room is amazingly hot.

The Nadi-Reader is already waiting. A Nadi-Reader is trained to read old-Sanskrit and to serve in the libraries only. He is the one who will out-read my Leaf although he does not speak English. This is what the translator is for.

There are two different bundles on the table. They're containing the Leafs. On top and on the bottom of each one is a wooden piece that holds the bundle together. The translator enters the room. We sit down.

"There are seven different roots of mankind", he explains. "You can recognize them on a certain coil within your thump impression", he points to his thump. I'm looking at mine.

"This particular angle is the sign that is painted on top of the bundle", he points out to one of the two bundles. There is indeed a strange sign on it. I'm looking at it and then again at my thumb.

"One bundle covers a certain time-frame when people from that particular root are coming to the library", he again points out to the bundle. "It is written when they will come. It is all written."

I'm nodding silently. When mankind is split into seven different roots and this library is in India where most of the people who search their Leaf are Indians, does that mean that most of my soul-relatives in this life are Indians?

The Reader takes the first bundle, uncovers it and puts the wooden pieces aside. Now I can see the Palm Leafs. They are right in front of me. I would just need to reach out and I could touch them. They are visibly old. The leafs are dry, some are broken on the sides. Exactly as it is told by the legend.

All of them are covered with long, knotted lines. That must be old-Sanskrit. No way he can read that!

He can. The Nadi-Reader starts chanting. Sanskrit is a chant. He chants a few data points to find out if my Leaf is there. The long awaited moment, it is here! Does my Leaf exist?

Within the incomprehensible chant I can hear him pronouncing my fathers and my mothers name. The translator turns to me and says:
"Your mothers name is Maria Margarete Sophie."
"Yes."
"Your fathers name is Burkhard."
"Yes."
"You've got a brother who is 2 ½ years older than you are. His name is Daniel."

"Yes."

"Your name is Antonia Katharina and you are born in Berlin on November 15, 1975."

"Yes."

"You went to a private school and you are working with horses. You have been married and your husband got killed in a motorbike accident."

"Yes."

"You are going to college and you study holistic medicine. You just past your exams in holistic psychology?"

"Yes."

"Your parents got divorced before you were born. Your father lives in a different part of Germany than your mother. Your father married a second time and is now divorced again. Your mother is in her second marriage and your brother passed his exams a few month ago and is now a doctor for allopathic medicine. He is living alone."

"Yes."

"And you are a musician."

"Yes."

"You are playing the piano", he smiles a warm and friendly smile.

"You never got over your husband's death yet."

Again, I'm nodding silently.

"This is why you came here."

This is why I came here.

"Your Leaf is here. You can wait outside. We'll get everything ready and read your life to you."

I get up, overwhelmed, moving the Indian way: In slow motion. No, it is no slow motion. What was time again? Illusion and Maya? I cannot sense time anymore. I'm amazed, speechless. I'm walking down the stairways, leave the library and step outside in the sun. I need to be outside right now. I need to move. I need to be all by myself.

My legs carry me down the street, past the little intersection right to the next corner. I can hardly feel anything around me. I just walk along the street but it doesn't feel like walking, it feels like the world is levitating and I'm floating.

So the legend is true. The handed down story is real. Time and space only exist within our limited consciousness. According to the legend it is real that we can immerse into the wisdom of all times, get information from there and write them down. The 'Akasha-Chronic' is just as real as the Rishis and the eternal Samadhi. The seer in 'The Alchemist' was wrong when he said that the future can't be known. It obviously *is* possible to know the future and to look into peoples lives.

Our existence is part of a much greater reality than I could have ever imagined. My entire life, everything that has ever happened, that will ever happen and that happens right now, just became a whole different meaning all together.

This moment is more intense than everything I've ever experienced. I can feel how it burns its impression deep into my soul. I know that its vibrations will influence me and my life from now until the end of time.

I cannot tell how long it takes until I get called back in. The translator comes out and waves. It now shall begin. We're going back to the same, small room.

There are all kinds of papers lying on the table now, handwritten notes, Palm Leafs, scribblings of the Nadi-Reader, all written in these long, knotted lines.

They will now reveal my life and my future to me. My history is written on these sheets. These old Palm Leafs, that almost fall apart, are holding the secret of my destiny.

I sit down. The Reading begins as well as my way into a whole new understanding of life entire.

13

The translator turns an old cassette player on. The Reading is being recorded and every paragraph will be directly translated as soon as the Nadi-Reader has finished.

"You were raised in West-Berlin", the translator begins.

"In your early years you went to a school which was named after one of the four evangelists. Later you went to a private school close to your home. Right after you finished you went to America, to Iowa. There you visited High School.

Your host family had many children. But none of them went to school, they all were schooled at home."

Every time the translator looks at me I confirm his statements by nodding.

"The house of your family was the only one within many miles. There was only one bus going once a day. You did not have a car or a license. The aloneness of this place had a very isolating character", he looks up and directly into my eyes. "You felt very alone and the loneliness made you suffer very much."

"Yes."

"When you came back from the US your hobby became your profession. You trained horses. Over the years you worked in different parts of Germany. Three years ago you stopped doing it full time. You went to college. You did not like how the animals were treated."

Yes, exactly. Everything he says is absolutely right.

"You are studying in Berlin. You are becoming a healer. You make a living out of your part-time job in the Olympic Stadium, training horses and the youngsters."

He looks at me and smiles. I'm still nodding.

"There is one horse you have an extremely good connection to. It is karmic. Winston."

What? They know Winston? How can this be possible?

It obviously is. But that is just the tip of the iceberg. Of course they know the story of my husband, how we met in the Olympic Stadium, that we got married and how he crashed and died. But all this is nothing compared to what follows then.

They also know what I think about my work. That I only study stupid medicine because I had no better idea what else to do. It is all written, explicitly.

They can describe very precise how I feel. They know about my pain, about my secret wish to die.

They know exactly how I am, how things are for me. They are telling me my deepest, innermost thoughts which I have not shared with anyone ever. But the Leafs know about them.

So, thousands of years ago my desolation was already decided for me? It was written before I was even born? Everything was already there, here, long before I existed as the person that I am today. Somewhere in the depth of time, one of the Rishis read my deepest and most personal life experience and wrote it down, so that I could find and read it thousands of years later.

I did not expect them to give such detailed information about my emotions. About facts, okay, but this is too much!

I always kept myself closed up. My inner world has been my secret garden to which no one ever got permission to. The closest friend has never been allowed to enter. It was my last hide-away, my salvation. This is where my deepest truth is kept, that only I know and that only I can understand. But these people here know all about it.

These hidden secrets are just now out-spoken by a man I have never seen before, who belongs to a different culture and whose English is hard for me to understand. He is more a stranger to me than all strangers I've met in my entire life combined.

I'm becoming aware of the fact that all the years of sadness were supposed to be a part of my life, right from the very beginning. My deepest pain was destined to be, ever since the Leafs were written 5000 years ago.

I feel like my shell is taken away from me. Now there is no place I can run to anymore. My hide-away is gone.

I'm confronted with all the feelings I tried to bottle up for so long. My business and work and studies were the crutch I walked on and they helped me to denial the truth of my grief about the loss of him, that cut me to the core and wounded me for life.

But now it is all out in the open.

It is sadness that is about to overwhelm me. The translator smiles as he is done. I feel exposed, naked and so weak that it seems a slight breeze could carry my away.

14

I'm sitting on my chair, motionless. I just sit there. The Nadi-Reader goes on. It is written that I will meet someone who will love me just for popularity reasons and if I would give myself into a long-term-relationship with this man my life will end in a disaster. I'm supposed to meet a German man between the age of 33 and 36, will get married, live in Germany and travel a lot.

"No, that's not true", I'm interrupting. The translator gives me a puzzled look, changes a confused view with the Nadi-Reader, looks back at me.

"That's what it says here", the translator replies.

"Can't be right", I'm consisting.

The tape recorder is being turned off. I don't know why but I'm absolutely sure that I will not get married to a German. Yesterday I had this clear vision of me living in India. Now this. I have no idea what power causes me to believe that I know my future better than the Leafs.

The Nadi-Reader rereads the paragraph again. Twice. It is written exactly what was told, but what he claims to be the truth leaves me with a weird feeling.

"Anything else?", the translator asks and smiles his heartwarming and sympathetic smile.

No. No objections anymore. I'm shaking my head.

How come, after all the secret and hidden truths which were just revealed, I'm interrupting the Reading and start a discussion? What kind of force took over and made me speak?

We leave the situation behind and continue. The tape player is turned back on.

My marriage will not be very successful. My hopes and dreams will not come true, my needs won't be met. I'll not be happy. Luck and happiness are not meant to be.

This is a terrible forecast. I want to cry but I can't. Is my life supposed to go on like this? Is everything supposed to stay that way until the end of my days? Will I run in circles forever? That can't be my life story! That cannot be all to the life I is given to me!

But what if it is? What, if this is just as true as everything else that's just been told? What then? Does it make sense to go on then? Is such a life worth living? Worth all the effort?

"You are meant to pay off karma and gain consciousness", the translator continues.

Nice. How?

"There are two chapters that are also part of the old scriptures. The chapters Shanti and Diksha", he explains. "Shanti means peace. The absence of all disturbances. The chapter contains the secret of past lives, your karma and also the remedial measures. Remedial measures are certain things you can do to solve karma and to heal your present life.

Diksha means 'energy of enlightenment'. It talks about the spiritual side of your karma and contains all things that have to be recognized and understood so you can regain your ability to happiness and inner peace."

He again smiles.

"Do you want us to read them to you?"

What a question! I came here, all the way, to receive every piece of information I can get to make my life better. I hope so much to find something that will help me to escape the circle of restlessness and self-destruction. I'm here to find a sense to life. I am here because I'm searching my treasure.

"Definitely!", is my answer.

"Wait outside then. We'll come and get you."

I'm going down the stairways one more time, leave the library and step outside. This time I turn to a little shop to my right. Someone sells coffee, tea and cookies.

The little stand is very dusty from the sandy street, just as the man working behind the counter. Laws on food hygiene doesn't seem to exist. Otherwise this little shag should not be allowed to be here. But that doesn't matter to me at all. On the opposite: Everything around seems to be so simple, kind of imperfect, that it makes my heart melt. I love it. Because imperfection has its own beauty. It makes life so real, so true, and it has a taste of freedom I barely see at home.

In Germany, someone with ideas has a real hard time though. This man sells the self-made pastries his wife bakes and makes tea and coffee for whoever comes to this place. He even serves in the library itself if someone asks for it. What a service! Impossible to have a little shop like this in my home country. The state, the country, the district or who knows would show up and impose so many restrictions that no business would be possible whatsoever.

Here, nothing has the touch of sterile perfection as it does at home. It is all so relaxed. Is that what causes the peace that is senseable all around?

I like the cookies and the Indian coffee. It is heated on an open flame and cooked with milk. It's sweet and gets served in little bowls, not bigger than an espresso cup.

I turn around and look at the library. My head is empty. All dreams I could possibly imagine would not reach the reality of possibilities hidden behind these walls. Maybe it is best if I would just let go of all the ideas I have in my mind and let life happen without me interfering.

The translator comes out of the library to also have a coffee. He and the man behind the counter are changing a few words in Tamil. The man who knows my life better than anybody else on this planet does not talk to me though. But he leans against the stand and looks right into my eyes. It's a deep look and he smiles this kind of smile which says that he knows about things I cannot even imagine.

I cannot tell who looks up to whom. On the one hand, he *knows* and I'm the one who doesn't. And he obviously enjoys the position he is in. On the other hand, I'm that strange being from another world and people here know that it is one of the richest and most developed one can live in.

Maybe it is the desire for this other world that speaks from his eyes; it is definitely desire for another world that speaks from *my* eyes.

We're looking at each other silently for a while.

The encounter with the translator of the Palm Leaf Library in Chennai won't be the last one. He comes a little closer to me and whispers:

"Don't make any plans for India because India has plans for you."

His view gets even more intense for a few moments than it has already been. He then turns around, points with his head towards the library and goes back in. I'm staying for a few seconds in front of the little stand and watch him leaving. I do not move. He doesn't turn around as he enters the wide open, wooden door to the place where he works and I still can hardly believe exists.

His voice still echos in my mind even after he is gone.

15

Shanti talks about a past life in England where I was born in a rich family. I was young and beautiful. The wealth and the beauty made me become a very arrogant lady. Shades of this arrogance are still visible up to this day. This is why people avoid me today just the way I avoided others back then. I showed off, was very cold-hearted and full of contempt.

Further I hit on my sisters husband who divorced her to marry me. My sister died early of sadness, pain and a heartbrokenness. This is why I lost *my* husband in this life and why I'm mourning. Now I'm the one who is about ready to die because of her broken heart.

Towards the end of my life I came back to my senses but it was too late to compensate the karma I had already created.

Right after the chapter Shanti is through, the remedial measures are being read. They tell about what I have to do to resolve my karma. It is written that I shall visit certain temples, attend certain masses and speak certain prayers. I'm also meant to go to an orphanage and serve a meal. Further I'm supposed to go on the streets and feed the poor. The locations where all that is to take place are specifically described. Also I should provide a certain amount of money for charity. When I first hear what the translator translates it almost feels as if he offers me to pay off my karma, but this time I keep my mouth shut. There is no doubt in my mind that I will do exactly as I'm told. This is what I'm here for.

Don't make any plans for India because India has plans for you.

The chapter Diksha will be read when all tasks are fulfilled. Then I'm supposed to come back and the last secrets of my Leafs will be laid out.

To be whole, to be happy, to be safe and sound - what beautiful ideas! What a gorgeous perspective! How far away is the memory of these feelings? How long is it ago that I bathed myself in them? Do I even really know them? I have no idea.

It is late afternoon as I'm leaving the library. The sun is still shining and it is still hot. The driver takes me back to the hotel. I'm going right up to my room and lay down on my bed. I can feel my heart beating. I'm still overwhelmed and my entire body is vibrating, resonating to my fascination.

I close my eyes. The heavens open up above me and I can see into the eternal universe where the stars rotate and where nothing is as is was before. Everything seems possible. Nothing seems to be impossible anymore. The world is a miracle and I'm a part of it. That's my last thought before I fall asleep.

In my dreams I'm sliding through the endless spheres of my memories. I see pictures of Germany, the US, India. Everything adds up to a colorful fresco made out of fragments of different parts of my life.

My life is a search. I'm in search of inner peace. I long to be one with the great principle of life, with the universe, with the holy spirit, with the essence. I tried to find consolation, tried all kinds of distractions to deceive myself, all kinds of amusements to not feel. But the distance between me and my goals only grew. I never found what I was looking for. I never reached satisfaction. I never experienced fulfillment.

It knocks. Alexander Bilson comes to the Hotel to have dinner. He is curious what the Nadi-Reader said. In all the years he lived in this country the call of the libraries never reached him. It is probably destined, pre-visioned and already written, who falls for the legend and who doesn't. It almost seems as if the people whose lives is written, follow the path to the library just like they follow their natural instincts. A trip to India is inevitable as soon as the message of the Leafs comes into ones life who is meant to hear the call. It seems almost as if their souls, through the deepest connection with the universe, know that it is them the mystery talks about, when it describes 'all the people whose life are written and kept in India'. Almost as if they know it will be their very personal story that is hidden there and that the revelation of the Palm Leafs will change their life forever.

16

When everything was always known, are suspicions, ideas, specific feelings toward certain things explainable than? Because we all carry a part of eternity within us. On the deepest level we are all one with the universe. Does the universal part of the soul knows? And has it always known the sense of our lives? Does this eternal part within ourselves knows our destiny? Are we all connected to the worlds wisdom and are we inspired by it without us being aware of it? Does our life configures itself according to what is already written in the Akasha-Chronic? Even though we don't have the ability to consciously read in it? But we are a part of the universe and connected to it. So, was our karma already decided for us before all time began? Maybe. Absolutely possible.

Only a very few Rishis could read in the worlds wisdom and there is probably no one who knows if there is still somebody today living on this planet who is able to do so. But there have been people who could do that. It is totally imaginable to gain insight into the universal spheres. It is possible to receive messages from the deepest level of consciousness on which we are one with eternity; and it is possible to hold on to them and to write them down without losing them, without them sinking back into the unknown, getting lost forever.

What a picture! What a vision! In what state of understanding did such humans live in and what was the higher sense of *their* existence? Were they messengers between different worlds, between different levels of awareness so that we get reminded that a higher knowledge than we know of exists? Were their lives supposed to remind us that it makes a difference on what we focus on with our minds and hearts? And that we are not so totally connected with our physical bodies than we, most of the time, think we are? Was the reality of their being supposed to give us a clue that we are actual spiritual beings, able to look into past and future lives?

I'm telling Alexander everything. The identification of my Leaf, the reading and the remedial measures I'm told to fulfill. He knows a tour guide who speaks English and Tamil, who is originated in Chennai and who can show me around. This way it would be possible for me to ask the priests in the specific temples for the specific prayers, to organize food for the orphanage and to feed the poor. Just as he finishes telling me all about this guy he takes his phone and calls him. A few moments later it is organized for someone to come all the way with me and to take me to the places I'm supposed to visit.

Everything happens by itself. It seems to be time for me to resolve my karma and to go through certain experiences. It seems that such experiences are literally waiting for me and want to be made. Life opens all its doors for me and all I have to do is pass.

Madras' Street with a Rikshaw in the back

17

The tour guide and the driver are already waiting for me when I leave my room the next morning. The tour guides name is Raj. It is eight o'clock in the morning and he takes me right to the first place I'm told to go.

We are leaving Chennai, driving for a while through the country side. It is wide, open Land, very dusty. A few palm trees are there and, again, all my living room plants. This is the right environment where they belong. They look beautiful. Much nicer than mine at home ever did and, most likely, ever will, too.

I'm supposed to go to the Agestheeswara Temple, to light candles and to pray to certain Gods.

I've no idea how to pray to these Gods. I've never done such thing before. Besides, the names of these Gods don't mean anything to me simply just because I have never heard of them so far. But even that is taken care of. The library staff gave a little, handwritten book to me where the meaning of all the Gods is described. It also includes the basics of Indian philosophy. I use the time I have in the car to read.

The Agastheeswara Temple is build for Lord Shiva and the planet Saturn. The booklet says: Lord Shiva symbolizes five different qualities: 1. Creation, 2. Destruction, 3. Illusion, 4. Redemption, 5. Preservation. Redemption means: Being free from all sins and being protected against Misfortune and losses. Illusion means: Being free of wrong beliefs and false ideas. It further says: The original tone of the universe is 'ohm'. The universe evolved out of this frequency. That means that the syllable 'ohm' is the spirit of all living things. 'Ohm' creates balance in the universe. Singing 'ohm' in prayers and meditations, all levels of the mind and the soul will come to harmony and balance. All fears will disappear and one will be protected by the universal spirit.

I never really understood that 'ohm' thing, but I've heard about it. I stopped meditating a long time ago. Some years back, I went through a phase when I did yoga but I never sang. 'Ohm' has never done anything to me really.

The text says that the destructive energy is a very powerful and important source because it prevents life. It is needed to destroy false Ideas and all things that keep the truth from being recognized. Disappointment is only the end of an illusion, even though it might be painful. But it is necessary from time to time if one wants to build his life on solid ground and not on quicksand, where every life construct will sink into before long.

I absolutely wish for my life-perspective to change. I absolutely hope that all the dark thoughts I'm thinking, all the dark feelings I'm feeling, will get destroyed. I don't want them anymore. I've had enough of them. I'm so tired of being depressed! I wish for something to come and to destroy them all, every single one. That is only possible with a very powerful force. I need to stop holding on to my sadness, I need to destroy the inability to accept my destiny. I wish for a new life. I want hope. I want my strength back.

Saturn is described as the 'guardian of transitions' between the 'now' and the 'future'. It symbolizes the border of time and space, the border of our ego. He reveals self-centeredness especially where it opposes the general well-being of nature. It forms the boundary of our consciousness. Its task is to make us understand that life exists within a greater context, in which everyone has its specific karma to fulfill; that freedom can only be attained through the acceptance of our responsibilities. Saturn supports the decision to willingly fulfill our personal destiny, to gain full awareness, to sacrifice egoistic desires in order to serve higher laws of nature, for the good of everybody.

Saturn is the symbol of limitation that we experience through the terms of our existence. This planet symbolizes the idea that everything we do today will have its consequences later, in this or in a future life. That means that we are responsible not only for ourselves, but also for the talents and strengths that are given to us.

Okay, so it is all about responsibility. Responsibility for our life, responsibility for our karma. Does that mean that I have to take responsibility for my destiny? Is our life our decision? Doesn't my life just happen to me or did I decide to have exactly the one I do, somewhere on a higher level? Did I want this karma so I can make certain experiences with which I pay off dues from past lives? Was I meant to go through the experiences I had so I can pay for the things I have done in earlier incarnations? Am I paying the price for not having been in harmony with the universal laws of love and grace?

I keep on reading. Now the book talks about Gods, the sanctities of India and their function.

Maybe the holy figures of Hinduism are comparable to the angels of Christianity. They are healers, transmitters of Gods holy will, heavenly messengers who are not God but not human either. They guarantee protection and they are symbols of purity and innocence. For some people they are the light that leads their way. They are subordinates to the highest power alone, they only bring good things in our life and answer our prayers. They have compassion, give comfort and consolation. And they are immortal.

Legends and stories often tell that angels and holy figures live in higher spheres, somewhere between earth and heaven. They cross the way of our life, bearing messages and open our eyes for new directions. They make us hope that everything can be overcome and that life always goes on somehow. Their existence gives us proof that higher forms of life exist and that death does not have the last word.

18

All the different spiritual ideas described by the Indian philosophy have one and the same goal: Enlightenment. This is to escape the circle of rebirth and karma. It is free for every human to choose the path they want to go. There is no right or wrong. Every life is similarly valuable and it is not up to us to decide what kind of experience, what lifestyle, what outlook of life, is good or bad. The scriptures just give an option to people who feel that the time for them is right to care consciously for their spiritual development.

Above the oracle of Delphi, that is the ancient site for pilgrims and prayers in Greece, which deemed to be the center of the world in its time, is written, engraved in stoned panels, the highest of all revelations: 'Know yourself'. To recognize and know oneself, to understand the laws of the universe, are described as *the final goals of life* and that self-recognition is for everybody, despite of class and race.

That means that we are supposed to find the answers for our problems inside of us and not outside of us. Everything is karma. Everything is predeterminated: Where I come from, who I am, what religion or believe I'm raised by. Everything is meant to be the way it is. Nothing is better or worse. Everything just exists the way it should be. No experience is useless. Every man goes through exactly the life-experiences that serves the soul the most on its journey to recognition, to knowledge, to enlightenment.

The Indian philosophies are teaching a way of self-realization. They are doctrines of salvation. In the Bhagavad Gita it says: The one who recognizes himself realizes God because God lives in each of us. And God is the truth. Everybody carries a part of it inside.

The Bhagavad Gita is the bible of India. Not only Buddhism but also Hinduism, which expresses itself through the variety of Gods and which is the most common religion in South India, is rooted in it. The opening word of the Bhagavad Gita says:

'Search, oh soul, the Eternal, because you are the temple of the living God and he, himself, lives within you as your own, eternal self'. The equivalent in the bible is written in the 1. Letter to the Corinthians, chapter 3, verse 16:

'Don't you know that you are Gods temple and that his spirit lives within you?'

God lives within every single human being. Not just in a few who claim to be chosen, or in certain groups.

God lives in every body and we have the power to destroy or to construct. It is in our hands to make life special and precious, to create it the way we dream of and to support each other in love. It is in our hands to stay with or against each other. It is our decision to create our future and to use the time that is given to us *for* us, not against us. We people are worth to be loved and whoever loves the people, loves God: 'Let us therefore follow after the things which make for peace and which will lift each other up' is what is said in chapter 14 of the letters that Paul wrote to the Romans.

We are the light of this world, and it is up to us to understand that.

19

It is noon by the time we reach our destination. Other than the way to the library which only took an hour, the temple is an entire day-trip. Lots of people are around. Many are visiting the temple. The visitors are Indians only. I cannot see white skin, I cannot see any other hair color than black. I'm the only foreigner and I'm accordingly observed by the masses. It is obvious: I'm a very exotic appearance for them. I can tell by the look in their eyes and by the views which stick on me just like before in the library.

I did not expect to be the only foreigner in such a lively part of this huge city. In Germany, especially in Berlin, one can see many faces of people from other nations. In Chennai, contrastingly, I see only Indians. I have not seen anyone else yet. And besides, here the misery is living right on the streets in an unexpected extend. People are still dying because of thirst and hunger.

There is no functional infrastructure. There are no schedules for buses or trains, no cabstands, no names of a single street on the corners. Absolutely nothing that gives possibility of orientation for someone who is not originated in this place. Even though English is the official language only a few people can really communicate in another language than their own. If I was alone I would be completely lost.

The temple is old and wonderful. The architecture is phenomenal. The building is shaped like a long triangle but without a top; it ends on three quarters with a platform. The building is approximately 25 meters high and richly ornamented with all different kinds of figures. They are all made out of stone and painted with the most beautiful colors. The variety within this fine sculpture work surrounding the facade is indescribable. The entire building is one huge piece of Art. But what I'm looking at is only the entrance.

I take my shoes off. That is the rule in India before entering a holy place. There are uncountable pairs of shoes in front. The sandals, that I purchased yesterday in a small shop on the roadside, immediately drown in this ocean of shoes, but I don't care much. I'm going barefooted through the huge gate and enter the temple.

Here are also masses of people around. Some are lying on the ground, rolling around on the concrete, humming in monotone voices different chants. Others walk around. Some are just standing or sitting somewhere, praying. All kinds of noises are coming from all kinds of directions. A little stand sells small cups, made out of clay, filled with wax. I just need to put a wick in it and I have a candle. The Indian version of a tealight. Raj, who stands the entire time protectively by my side, gets a few of these lamps for me that the library wants me to light. Then he shows me the way inside where a priest just performs a mass.

There are no benches. There is no altar. And there is no order whatsoever. Order seems to be nowhere in this country. So why should it be especially here in this place?

A big crowd of people is staying, packed like sardines, in the middle of the hall. The priest is someone who looks almost exactly like all the others. The only difference to all the others that makes him recognizable is, that he is staying right in the middle and everyone else around him. Many of them brought fruits, flowers or candles. First he blesses the small gifts, then he turns to the circle of people around him, holding a tray in his hands that he passes around. There are different powders on it. A candle is burning. The powders are colors which are supposed to be put on the forehead. The candle is for the blessing. Comparable to a holy communion in a Christian church the priest goes around and hands the tray to one after another.

Everybody paints a line on his forehead. Next, everyone holds his hands over the candle and goes three times back and forth between the candle and the forehead, just as if they wanted to put the light from the flame right between their eyebrows. This spot is meant to be the third eye which is supposed to open the inner sight. I'm watching the scene and immediately remember: Hinduism is all about enlightenment. The rituals of their masses are, of course, based on exactly that objective.

I am observing all these rituals, knowing now what to do. The tray is handed to me. For the first time I paint a line on my forehead and do the ritual with the candle. All the people around fix me with their eyes. They do not turn them away from me, not even as I'm done and the tray is already past over to the next person. They look at me as if I was an alien who flew, directly from out of space, right into their temple. I'm the attraction of the day.

Afterwards I'm walking through these huge, gigantic halls. There are different corners with all kinds of different holy figures around. After a while I find a quiet place and sit down right on the floor. I close my eyes. It is unbelievable: Even though all these people are around, this strange kind of peace is perceptible that I sink into immediately.

My thoughts are clear and pictures arise. I see lots of people. People who are levitating weightlessly through the universal space, each one shining from within. I'm right with them. We are all made out of a transparent substance. But it is no glass, it is something organic.

We're all connected with each other. We can sense us. We can read our thoughts. We can feel one other. There is no planet anymore, just us and the sphere we are floating in and which is infinite. It is peaceful. Perfect harmony of our thoughts and feelings fulfills the situation.

We are all part of one big light we carry inside, that keeps us alive and that makes us shine. When only one of us loses his light, we will all loose it and eternity will fall into darkness. Almost like one of these fairy lights on a Christmas tree, where you have to turn one light and all the others go on or off.

We are all one, but also different parts. We are all of one kind but not the same individual. We belong to one family, we all have the same appearance and carry the same light within; we belong together, we are somehow attached, but we are not touching physically. We are bright beings, floating through the endless space, somewhere in the depth of time.

I emerge out of my deep thoughts, open my eyes and look around. Even though I see real people I'm not recognizing them as what they are. It is like I can feel them around me. It feels that our consciousness is connected with each other, just as if the one universal light shining from within the center of the all, shines through all of us.

So, Shiva destroys illusion. What, now, is the illusion? My vision or what I see in the outer world?

Is it an illusion to believe that I'm alone? Is it an illusion to believe that we have nothing to do with each other and the thoughts and feelings of others are none of my business? According to my vision there is this level on which we are all connected. According to what I just saw it is real that each one of us carries a life-light inside and that we are all parts of this one light that flows through us, feeds us, keeps us alive, makes us be.

We are our orientation. We are our family. We are the carriers of the universal light, the temple of the living Gods who live in all of us. Exactly as it is written in the Gita.

We are the lights of life. And the life that we are allowed to be a part of is holy.

Front of the Temple

20

The next day Raj takes me to an orphanage. We talk to the staff and organize the food. As far as I know, an orphanage is a facility where children live. But here, every home for homeless people or for people without relatives is called an orphanage. The one Raj takes me to is a home for elderly women who don't have family, which is very rare in India. We are talking to the matron, Mrs. Mehra Kumar, and arrange the food for the next day.

It is Raj who talks to the owner of a restaurant and explains to him what we are planning to do. It is Raj who organizes the transport of the food. And it is Raj who indicates the driver to pick me up on time so we get to the orphanage before the transporters are there. I have no idea how I could have done all this without his help. Everything, without exception, really everything seems to be ready and fully organized, so I can fulfill the mission that is waiting for me for the past thousands of years.

Mrs. Kumar and the doctor of the house are already waiting as I arrive. The doctor introduces himself as Mr. Balashaktisubramanium. Ever since I will never be able to pronounce his name, not even after another 5000 years of chanting Palm Leafs, I smile and secretly decide to just call him 'doctor'.

They show me around. It is a simple house, no carpets, no wallpaper, no color on the walls. There are only women here, all 70 years of age and older. They are all very thin, including the doctor and the matron.

We enter the room where the old women sleep. Everybody sleeps on the blank, stoned floor. They are thin and scraggy and they are all suffering hunger. I can tell by their stature, by their deep sunken eyes, their lean arms, by the bones of their fingers that are covered with skin. But as I look at them I cannot feel any pain, no struggling with destiny, no sadness except of my own.

As soon as the old women see me, they have tears of joy in their eyes and bless me. Because they are so happy and grateful for the food I bring. I cannot sense the slightest sign of envy, no jealousy, no aversion against me at all.

In India, every human being is holy, no matter if rich or poor. Not like in Germany, where someone who loses his job for whatever reasons, falls out of the system and needs help, is marked by the society as a looser.

But yet there are also such kind of people back home who believe that they are entitled to be taken care of by the system, and the state is bound to finance their personal desires such as cars, housing, television, mobile phones. All that is included in the state doll. As rich as Germany is, everyone has the right to possess these things by law, employed or unemployed. Now, many of the people living on the states support system complain the most. I know that well. From the Potsdamer Table. Every Saturday.

Such support system doesn't exist here. Especially not in a comparable dimension. These people are far away from a lifestyle we are used to. They are really poor. That's why they know about the value of a meal much more than we do, who grew up with nice kitchens and full refrigerators.

Everyone here knows that only by accepting the personal destiny, karma can be fulfilled. The future of the soul is basically decided by their respect, acceptance and love towards life and their serenity through all the experiences they are presently meant to go through. And the question is: Does one holds on to love and care for others, even though life's circumstances are adverse? Is the soul filled with peace despite all difficulties of ones life circumstances? Or is the mind restless and so entangled with matter that personal happiness depends on outer conditions?

The little book describes detachment as to be the first step on the way to enlightenment; detachment from things, from personal desires, from material goods. And that loving service to mankind is the sense of all life, no matter what part of society one is rooted in. The more one understands about the essence of love, the closer the soul comes to its own liberation from the circle of rebirth and karma. In the end the soul will be released from all sorrows of the world.

The people here are just alike that. I can feel that they are living on their believe in this philosophy. They are full of gratitude. They seem to be satisfied, content, unbelievably: Happy. Happier than I have ever been.

21

The doctor takes me to the house owned clinic. The clinic of the house is a room, maybe 5 x 7 feet, which looks more than the bicycle cellar in my brothers basement. It is muddled, dark and dirty. But that is all they can afford and the doctor, as well as Mrs. Kumar, are proud to present that this facility even has an own clinic. I don't let my thoughts show. Instead I keep smiling, just as it is common here.

The transporters arrive, the food is being delivered. In their minds I'm a rich woman that I never thought I was but which I obviously am compared to these people. In Germany I'm living the life of an average college student: Small 1 1/2 bedroom apartment, no car, but a land line and internet. And, of course, the basics of every German: Bed, cupboards, desk, functionable kitchen and a bathroom where everything works properly. Compared to them I'm definitely rich, no doubt.

The food that comes and which is supposed to feed 120 people doesn't cost me more than an average dinner for two people in my home country. That is affordable even for a college student, who doesn't earn very much on the side. The women here are treating me like a saint who got send to them only to put food on their plates.

Being the 'rich German' - an extremely wired feeling, especially because it absolutely doesn't match my personal understanding of me and my life.

Just as the transporters open their doors two young women are rushing hastily around the corner, both also very skinny, to unload the vehicles. The quick view into the kitchen that I catch as Mrs. Kumar takes me to the dining hall, tells me that the food is being stretched. They're putting water in it. This way it may be enough, not only for one, but maybe for two or three days or even the entire next week.

A bell rings. That means lunch is about to be served. Women come from all different directions. Some are limping, some lean on each other for support.

The wooden tables are without any place setting. Each woman brings a leaf from a palm tree, that is squared and cut to the size of a plate. Even though these leafs are not 500 years old, I can see that they are not used for the first time. They're the everyday pads, given that there is something to eat every day. That is all; there are no more dishes than that. There is no cutlery, nothing. People in India don't only eat with their fingers out of tradition, but also simply because they can't afford anything. Dinnerware is for the rich.

Bowls with rice are handed to me which I'm supposed to serve. I'm going slowly through the rows. Many of the old women are crying over their luck to be endowed so richly. Some even get up and bless me.

To see so much poverty makes me modest. And to see, on top of that, in what kind of doubtless harmony these people accept their destiny makes me humble. I don't know if I would have called myself demanding or ignorant, but right in this moment I understand that I'm exactly that. Presumptuous. Demanding. Greedy. Believing that I'm entitled to receive a certain amount of happiness and that the wealth of a country like Germany is the basic standard. It embarrasses me to see these poor people in such solitude, in such gratitude, so filled with appreciation and joy, without wrath, without any disgrace over their poor, hand-to-mouth life.

When I look at me through their eyes I see a rich girl that has nothing because she cannot recognize the great gifts that are given to her, coming from this world sated with luxury; poor and broken because she has no idea how lucky she is.

How come that I seriously think the world is meant to make me happy and that it has to fulfill my personal desires? How come that I think it is my right to be angry only because life doesn't go exactly the way I want it to go? How can I believe I have nothing and my life is worthless only because I lost someone? Because the same time I'm not lacking anything and my life is overfilled with possibilities to design my future any way I want to. I know that I will never suffer hunger; that I will always be taken care of. I know all that, and I understand how blessed I am the moment I look into these deep, peaceful eyes. I just right now realize how much is given to me and that I could never really see it.

"Do you want something to eat?", Mrs. Kumar asks. She points to two empty chairs in the next room and puts immediately a palm leaf on the table. She also puts one for herself and serves rice and vegetables.

"You look so happy", I'm telling her as we sit down.

"I *am* happy", she replies, "why should I not be happy?"

What am I supposed to say now? I can't say something like: 'Because you don't have much to eat', or: 'Because you have to sleep on the floor', or: 'Because you have to live in such poverty'.

"You mean because we are not as rich as you are in the western countries?", her voice is full of contentment.

I would have never wanted to say it that way, but: yes, of course I wonder how one can not only be so happy in such circumstances but also be so fulfilled like the people here. What do they have that I'm lacking?

I don't answer. Silence. She recognizes that I'm thinking and doesn't speak for a while. I'm watching her using her fingers to eat. She's very skilled. I'm trying as good as I can to also do so. After a while she turns to me:

"I believe the entire sense of us being here is the service to others", she looks at me and smiles as if there was nothing greater than what she just told me.

"Every form of selfishness creates new karma and extends sorrows. This is why egoism is always without any sense", she explains.

"The light that leads a person from within is always love. Nothing else is required. There *is* nothing else. No one will be capable of anything more. While serving others, the heart opens. Here we find the highest materialization of mankind possible; In the service to others we have humanity close to its own fulfillment and right by its very purpose. I believe in this", she looks at me and her eyes gleam as she continues:

"With a smile that I gift I'm serving love. When I'm listening open-hearted to a friend, I'm serving him in love. With understanding, and not judgment, I'm serving in love. With consideration, not with complaints, I serve in love. It is very easy, you know?" I'm nodding.

"Giving oneself into the great, God-like oneness doesn't mean anything else but to open up to the feeling of love and care and to let it flow through your entire being. What can there be greater than that?

Here, one will find healing and wholeness. Here, one will find the peace that nothing outside of us will ever be able to supply. Here, the veil lifts and the one and only sense of life becomes visible: Compassion.

Through love serves one another. That's what it says in the letter to the Galatians, right? And in the first letter of Peter: *Everyone serves one another, each with the gift he has received*.

Everything is here. Just use the things that are given to you. It is all written, no matter if in the New Testament or in any other holy scripture of any other culture. The essence is always the same: *Through love serves one another*.

I believe in this. And that is why I provide my service to others. This kind of service holds its own reward. It gives inner richness, happiness and true peace of mind. It is the service that we are all empowered to do. It is the service that everyone can do, anywhere at any given time. And most of all: It is a purpose that is really worth living for."

How lovingly she talks. How fulfilled her eyes are. How smooth her voice is.

I'm close to believing myself that I'm on another planet. The purpose of these peoples lives is so clear, their believe is so pure, their solitude seems to be so naturally given. It is so true what she says. I've heard and read such words thousands of times, but written texts always have the character of phrases and sentences accurately planned. They don't reveal if they came spontaneous, neither if they are put into practice. But she talks without thinking or searching for words, speaking out loud what we might consider as wisdom. And she doesn't even do it consciously but naturally, just telling me how she lives.

While she's talking I'm trying to eat rice and veggies with my pure fingers. It sadly doesn't work very well.

Mrs. Kumar, watching me, being kind enough to pretend not to see how childish I look. She, on the contrary, uses her fingers so proficient that they are not even soiled.

"We always eat with our fingers. It tastes better that way", she, smiling.

Understand. Just try to explain that to my mother who invested years of sweat and hard work to make me giving up on exactly what I am doing right now. All of her efforts, wasted, within one single meal.

22

My sense of time is changing because my perspective of life is changing. My senses are bringing back some of the taste and smell of my early years I can only remember from afar. It is the first time in so long that I have serious interest in the things around me. Is it only me who withdrew from life so that my perception was fogged and my senses were dull; or is it us, the people of the western hemisphere, who are so supersaturated that our feelings are deadened and our lives are deserted?

My lifestyle, that I have just become so used to, now seems to be strange, far away and long ago. Have we lost all ability to value our things?

Our problem is that we can't make up our mind, within all the possibilities we have, within all the open doors there are. We can't decide which is the 'dream job', the 'dream vacation', the 'dream partner'. Everything is replaced as soon as it doesn't suit our desires anymore. We think about the clothes we wear, the hair color we want to have and the newest fashion that is declared to be important to follow up with. Trivialities are gaining more and more significance.

In the end, the punishment of a life where one can have everything they always wish for is, that the personal desires and expectations are always increasing in relation to what is supplied: This means, they can never be met.

The price of our wealth is a certain delusion that makes us value the things we have much more than even recognizing who we really are. We believe that we are nobody because we don't owe enough stuff; we believe we are not worth anything because we don't have a high payed job, and we are afraid to be denied by society if we don't fit in the average definition of a citizen defined by law. We possess things, but can't see the value of what we actually have. We may think about poverty in the world once in a while only to turn around and complain that on today's pizza the ham is missing. Or that the full paid vacation is over. Or that it's raining outside.

We tend to measure success by the amount of our income and by the size of our cars, but totally forget about every kind of humanity. To be modest is not a parameter for success. Success, in the western world, means to own and to possess. It means to have followed a certain path within the structure of a system one is meant to be conform with. Sympathy does not count to the things desirable. Kindness and compassion are not considered to be achievements.

The descriptions of love and grace, that are handed down by the holy scriptures, do almost sound like pure irony when looking at the atrocities Christianity brought into this world. An uncountable amount of people in the European latitudes got tortured and killed throughout centuries. The average person in Germany is almost ashamed call him- or herself spiritual, if not embarrassed, when looked at with ridicule by others. Even though the New Testament and the message of Jesus is full of love and kind-heartedness and very spiritual indeed. But it is not very surprising, either, after what thy holinesses of Christianity, or better: The ones self-proclaimed to be the holinesses of Christianity, made out of it and did in the name of Jesus and the 'Holy Scriptures'. A religion that brought so much sorrow and destruction over a country and that destroyed entire cultures can't impossibly be rooted in brotherly love and compassion. They did not only annihilated the Heathenish and Celtic culture but also almost erased the entire native American race in the gigantic country, which today is known as the 'United States Of America'. The leaders of such an institution can impossibly carry the message of hope and humanity into the world. That's out of question.

Through the burning of the witches, where they randomly killed everyone who didn't swear to their God - man, women and children, a butchers-party in the name of the Bible, thrown by the Christian church - we are all deprived of our believe and trust in Jesus teachings. Our trust in compassion, empathy, feeling for others, is taken away from us all. They made it extremely hard for everyone to find an access to the message that is revealed through the Bible. Our original, Celtic culture is taken away from us and we are betrayed over the message of Jesus Christ. Because it got distorted, perverted and misused, favoring war and murder until today.

On the European continent, a whole different culture was dominant. Where did it go? When these so called 'disciples' of Jesus carry so much love within, why do these cultures don't exist anymore today? Because they are not able to allow anything else besides them and believe that nothing except themselves has a right to live on this planet. We all will see the results of such mind set in the days to come.

How many uncountable inquisitors, who haven't been nothing else but mass murderers, excused their behavior with the Bible? The Heathens were just condemned as Godless, also the Celtics. 'Non-believers' were told to be barbarians and the aborigines of America supposedly wild animals, which were declared `free to be killed`, with the full approval of the highest authority of the church.

How can such things be happening in 'God's name' and the same time it is being explained that 'God is love'? When that is love, God's love, than the word 'love' must have a definition which has nothing, absolutely nothing, in common with what is understood by love throughout ordinary people. So this kind of 'love' the church is talking about can't be anything that is worth achieving, nothing worth caring about.

This kind of disruption with their original believe never happened to the Indians. Here, the Christians did not kill the way they did in Europe. The horror of the crusades and the massacres including burning women, never reached this country, never undermined this culture. The believe-system of the

Indians doesn't justify to destroy entire nations. Their spirituality is rooted in a philosophy of enlightenment. It describes a way to self-realization. Nothing else.

The Christian church still denies its holocaust today. They have never said sorry once. They never asked for forgiveness, they never regretted.

And it still denies science, which tells us that on a quantum physical level, the last substance of all matter is light – visible and invisible. All life and every piece of matter is a form of vibration. Every quantum is reacting to the others and the interaction changes according to how things vibrate to each other. And ever since we human beings are part of this universe and made out of the same substance like everything else, this law of interaction is just as relevant for us as it is for matter.

We all are part of this one wholeness. This is where we come from. This is what we are made out of. And this is where we'll go back to. The ancient holy scriptures, Indian, Celtic, Heathenish, are telling us exactly that since thousands of years.

The holy scriptures, not only of India, are talking about the structure of the universe, different levels of awareness and the dimension of our consciousness.

Everything in the solar system is subject to a circle of becoming and passing. This is being observed and noticed for thousands of years. So, why should the soul, of all things, not be integrated in this circle that continues forever and keeps repeating itself over and over again? Just like inhaling and exhaling, day and night, the seasons that come and go and start over right from where they began, year after year, the soul is dying and reborn life after life. That's how it is with everything, everywhere in the whole universe.

The single tree symbolizes the circle of life the best of all living things. It outlasts all times for a while. During summer it is in full abundance, full opulence. During winter, with blank branchwood and without leafs, appearing like a skeleton, blooming back in spring, going on and on with this cycle until it finally, one day, passes off for good.

Even the movement of the planets is cyclical and they run on a predefined orbit. The central planet of our solar system will burn out one day and the planets will fall back into the darkness of the cosmos which they once arose from. Then, every single bit of life that has ever seen the face of this world will have never existed.

What is the sense of all this? In the holy scriptures of all cultures is written that the sense behind everything existing is the service to others in love. That is the reason why we are here. They talk about not to put the material side of life in the first place, but to direct the focus to what lives *within*. Some call it the 'holy spirit', some the 'soul', 'mind', there are many names already given to it.

But all scriptures are claiming that this invisible part that lives within and keeps us alive, that breathes us, is the part born right out of eternity. They claim that this part is related to the eternal. And that this part has the same essence like the universe itself, being holy, living eternally.

Eternity is described as a sphere that has been there before the world began and that will be there after the world will end. And the world *will* come to an end, just as everything in it will come to an end on a certain point of time. The principle is always the same: Arising – disappearing - arising, up and down and up, inhaling – exhaling - inhaling, life - death – life, life after life until it's all over.

The Buddha says, that true contentment only comes from wishlessness, and not from the fulfillment of all desires. Ja, he even says, that the more vehement someone desires something, the more desires one has and the harder one craves for them coming true, the further away he turns from true richness of life, true peace of mind.

May we recognize and know ourselves. May we understand that we are a such precious parts of this incredible universe. May we know that we are all one. So that our souls wont save one day on our richly filled and supersaturated tables.

23

There must be more than what I have seen and experienced in my life so far. I'm safe, I don't suffer any sorrow, I've been successful and loved. But when I look back I can't feel any satisfaction, no fulfillment. On the opposite: I feel empty and my life seems to be meaningless.

Today we'll go downtown, right to the heart of Chennai. I'm picked up at about 10. We are going to a mall, a huge shopping center.

The drive through Madras is very long but I'm not bored. I see many, very small shops along the streets.

Shops along the streets in a quieter part of the Town

Yamaha-Specialist, Madras

They don't have entrances, just small desks on which only one single person finds space to stay. Houses, small businesses, rows of stores and street hawkers, cars, rickshaws, family reunions on motorbikes and cows. It is a hopeless tohubohu. The streets are completely crowded.

None of the vehicles has a catalytic converter. The rickshaw-motors are two-strokes and rattle like little lawnrakers. The mopeds are two-strokes, too, and rattle just likewise. Dogs are no two-strokes but are barking. Cows are not barking but appear in small groups and dally around the main streets, unimpressed by it all. In the open air I'm close to suffocating; Then again, other people are sleeping in the middle of this jam-packed craziness. They are lying on the sidewalk, right on the concrete or directly on the median strip. They are lying there! They are just lying there, sleeping!

They are almost all men. Raj explains to me that they have to work so much that they just sleep where they are. A 40 hour week and full payed vacation, like we have in Germany by law, is something these men can only dream about.

"Madras' citizens are used to the pollution and such a lot of noise", he says.

Is it possible to get used to this amount of noisiness? The idea of getting used to it seems to be totally absurd, but this is how it is described to me. They don't need a bed, no comfortable mattresses, no extra quiet rooms to find peace. That is a thing of the western world. People like us depend on all these luxuries, believing that without them we can't exist. What kind of drama takes place when someone can't sleep? Sometimes the washing machine of a neighbor two stories down is enough to be the cause of anger and sleepless nights, or the partner who is snoring. Marriages are getting divorced because of that! What a grotesque thought by looking at the view just described.

We are reaching the mall. The driver stops at the end of the sidewalk, which is edged with a metal fence so the wild traffic and the masses of people won't interfere.

The open air sauna runs on full power. I'm walking slowly towards the mall. On the side of the fence a man is sitting on the walkway. He is half naked, only covered with a small piece of cloth around his loins. He reaches out to the ones walking by, with scraggy arms, and begs for a few rupees.

The man is so scrawny that I immediately know, without needing to put any further thoughts into this, that he will die right where he sits, sooner or later. Maybe not today, maybe not tomorrow. But will he still be alive next week? Not certain. To think further down the line, and imagine him still being here next month, almost feels like me imagining him in his next life. If not some kind of miracle happens, this man does not have another 20 days to live. A few rupees a day will not keep him from dying. It may delay it for a bit, but it won`t stop death from coming.

My steps are slowing down. Driving to a mall in Madras may include passing by dying people. Welcome to India.

I'm giving the man some money. But even all the money I own cannot take the misery away from Indias streets. Maybe it will help the man over a few days and the generously counted 20 days will unexpectedly expand to 25. But it won't be much longer than that, for none of the beggars here. Because he is only one of so many, that I can't count them.

I want to sit down on the steps leading up to the mall but they are made out of black stone and the sun pours directly down on them. They are so baked out that it hurts me to just touch them. That is why I'm going through the entrance right into it.

Inside I basically find the same chaos as outside, only in a more compacted form, without noisy cars, without cows. There are stoned fringes everywhere. I sit down on one.

I know about hunger in the world. I know about poverty in India. But to see it and to experience it directly is just as if I've never ever heard or read about it before, just as if the reality of it didn't even exist in my mind. The entire world knows about these circumstances, but actually we know them not. We just don't know them. We don't know poverty, so the concept of poverty doesn't exists in our minds. And we are not able to imagine poverty. Pictures on TV and articles in newspapers ain't enough to really know.

A child comes towards me. I'm raising my view. It stops and stands still. Petrified. Stares at me for a few seconds, turns around and runs away. At least it didn't scream.

I look around and notice that I am, again, the only white human being around. Maybe the child has never seen someone with white skin before? Although there are all kinds of shampoo bottles, cookie boxes and toilet paper wrappings, where pictures of white people are used for advertising. Bright skin is a good marketing strategy that sells. But the little guy probably feels like I do; I'm just as unreal for him as poverty here is unreal for me, even though I have seen it thousands of times before and I can't say I didn't know about it. But it *is* new for me.

What will these impressions do to me? What will these experiences do to my life? What happens here with me? I want to get up but I can't. My knees are weak, my legs are shaking. I'm dizzy and my heart is beating hard. I close my eyes and see myself in free fall, somewhere into the depth of a roomless darkness. I'm falling; I'm sinking. Into bottomlessness. Into endlessness. Just like a stone falling into water, with no ground to it.

I'm sinking.

And sinking and sinking.

I'm sinking into the depth of an unknown world. Will there be something waiting for me at the end? Is there an end? Or will this fall take forever, will I sink endlessly, will I lose myself somewhere in the eternal darkness and get insane after all?

My life falls into pieces. The borders of my consciousness are blurring. Everything I knew and that has been some kind of orientation for me fades. The understanding I had about life so far vanishes just as much as these new impression get to me. Who am I? What kind of life do I have?

Is there anything in my life that is important? That really has a meaning? I can't see anything. Can't realize anything. My life is nothing. I own a lot, but I'm nobody. I have things, but I don't know who or what I'm supposed to be. There is no purpose, no direction, no goal. There is nothing. Only the endless fall into the nothingness of all times.

I'm letting go. Taking deep breaths and releasing my entire self every time I exhale, release the fragments which are left of it. I'm washing them out of my body, giving in to the deep emptiness in which I'm drowning with my entire being. I let go and let go and let go. There is no other way if I don't want to go crazy on myself. Letting go, over and over again, until everything is released and I feel empty.

Now it is quiet. Absolutely quiet. I just got down to the bottom of my being and just sit there, staring into nowhere, not seeing anything.

I don't feel like walking through the mall. I don't feel like doing anything anymore. I just want to sit here forever, until the end of time, and absorb the stillness inside of me, to give myself into it, to immerse in it. The long awaited peace, it finally came down on me, right here, in a place where I would have never ever possibly expected to find it.

Everything I'm looking for is right here, right inside of me. A small window opens up and eternity is sensable. I'm flooded by it. I'm right in the moment of the eternal now. My awareness lifts its boundaries and I see the infinite universe we are a part of. Everything is an endless circle. Nothing is permanent. Only the transition between life and death, becoming and elapsing.

All that is, is subject to permanent change. Even thoughts. Even moments of fulfillment, like this one.

I must have sat here quite a while, because the sun stands much deeper than it did when we arrived. I'm walking back to the car. The beggar is still in the same spot. Raj is waiting for me by the car and smokes. The driver is sleeping.

"Did you have a good time?", he asks with a calm voice.

"Sure did", I reply, getting into the car, closing my eyes and remain silent on the way back to the hotel.

24

The next task I'm meant to fulfill is already waiting for me the next morning. Again, we're going to a temple. It is the Partha Sarathy temple, also outside Chennai.

I'm supposed to pray to certain Gods. While we drive down there I'm doing my research through the little book as I have done before, trying to understand what the meaning behind these personifications of different Gods mean.

The temple is far outside the city and the drive takes several hours. Raj knows exactly where we're going. It seems like he knows all ways and every single place throughout the entire region. No matter if malls, temples, orphanages, he just knows where these things are to be found.

It says that I'm supposed to pray to Lord Vishnu and Devi Lakshmi. 'Vishnus' is an old Saskrit term, meaning 'the all-pervading'. He is the warden of humanity and the God of preservation. It says that he is responsible for the maintenance of a certain cosmological order. He incarnates to maintain the cosmological order again and again, as a human or as an animal, just when the worlds order is about to lose its balance.

Creatures like that are called 'Avataras'. It is very common that disciples of Vishnu, who are familiar with the philosophy and the content of the Bible, admire Jesus Christ as The Messiah. Because the Bible describes Jesus as the rescuer who will appear at the end of all ages to save the world.

The wife and sustaining power of Vishnu is Devi Lakshmi. She is the God of happiness and beauty, donor of richness and well-being, of greatness, harmony and abundance. And she is a protector of plants. She appears in different ways: Once she is the personification of knowledge, once she is the personification of the earth, to than appear as the personification of success, achievement and perfection. Her name 'Lakshmi' is etymologically related to the word 'lux', which is Latin and means 'light'; to the English term 'luck' as well as to 'Lucia', the saint of light. The Lucia festival was celebrated in the early middle ages, honoring the winter solstice, the turning point of the tides, the every years rebirth of all life.

In each incarnation of Vishnu, Devi Lakshmi appears by his side. When Vishnu incarnates as Krishna, she appears as his friend Radha. When he incarnates as king Rama, she is his wife Sita, or even Maya, the governor of illusion, of ignorance and of the delusion of duality.

The maintenance of a certain cosmological order in life doesn't mean anything else but to be in harmony with all things. And to be in harmony with all things means to be in harmony with nature, to be in harmony with God.

Paulo Coelho mentioned that. I've read it in the plane. A few days ago I've thought to be ages away from any kind of harmony or oneness, but the less I'm entangled with my egoistic self and the more I open up to the world around me, the more I can feel the harmony with my surrounding, with things, with nature.

Was that deep-touching feeling, which I experienced yesterday, what is described as `closeness to God`? Have I been close to God? Is that what I'm longing for?

As I'm getting out of the car I step into the same humanitarian disaster and poverty. It is a suburb of Chennai. No crazy traffic is there. There are hardly Vehicles. The streets are plain sand, most of the houses are not solid. The 'houses' are basically made out of wooden sticks, cloths are stretched over them, people living underneath.

Beggars are sitting in front of the temple, just as thin and low-in-weight as all the others I have seen so far. Their skin is just as crinkled, their eyes just as pleadingly. Almost everyone I look at is starving to death. Maybe it is their hope, to be rescued and to find happiness in higher dimensions of existence, that keeps them alive? The philosophy says: When they just accept their destiny they'll live, at least, in peace with their karma. What else do they have, except of the believe that being in harmony with the things and all circumstances is *the* way to enlightenment? And that enlightenment is the one and only thing that has the power to release them from coming back life after life? What else is there for them?

I try to imagine: Being in harmony with *that* kind of life? Could I be? Would that be possible for me? I don't know.

For a fraction of a second some pictures from my own life are flashing up in my memory and I immediately wonder how I could have ever been unhappy.

A little, crippled dog comes limping towards me. I'm grabbing a few cookies from my pocket and hold them in its direction. He rips them out of my hand and gulps them down so hastily, that I have to pay attention not to get bitten in my fingers.

His leg is broken, but to get some cookies he limps right across the entire street, just as if nothing else than them exists, just as if there would never be anything else.

25

My thoughts are spinning in my head and I'm not able to get a hold of a single one. Everything seems to happen the same moment, past and future don't seem to exist anymore and the pictures in front of my eyes are a mixture of impressions and emotions.

I'm walking towards the entrance of the temple. The terminology of a 'fair cosmological order' just withdraws from the sphere of my understanding. But, on the other side, my personal unhappiness vanishes the same time I see these people dying around me. It is absolutely understandable that they believe in some sort of savior, who will come to save the world and to reestablish the fair cosmological order again; because this is the glimmer of light and hope throughout such a lifespan.

I can absolutely imagine where such hope is coming from: It is the deep certainty of starvation which is inevitable. These people are eye in eye with their own death. Are they afraid? Are they sad? Are they yearning for it? Believing it to be their salvation, hoping that death holds the solution for their sorrows and peace is waiting for them?

What kind of pain does one suffers whose life leads him right in front of the doorsteps of an Indian temple, where he is destined to die? I can't even really tell what kind of pain one suffers who is not directly affected but is walking by, watching people suffering such a destiny.

To live surrounded by so much poverty has its own burden. The chance to fall into this kind of misery and to maybe starve on the open streets one day is there, waiting, everywhere, at all times. If one fails to work continuously for his daily bread, than such a future is inescapable. It is already decided: Whoever is not able to care for himself, dies.

No wonder that the bond of a family has a totally different meaning than it has in the country I'm coming from. The fact of having family or not decides, in case of doubt, about life and death. There is no system of the government whatsoever that is able to feed all these people. The population of India exceeded already one Billion. It is impossible to feed all of them out of one food counter like the one I got to know. This catastrophe requires much more than that.

That the money in this world is not evenly distributed is an open secret. India is a state with nuclear power.

The same time, hunger kills hundreds of people every day and death is going around wherever lays eyes on. In Germany the system is out of balance, too, but to the other side. We're all taken care of, no one has to suffer hunger or poverty, but everybody constantly complaints. There is this absurd situation that some families, where none of the members has a job, get more money from the government than a worker who earns his income with daily work and sweat. It happens that people who earn their living with regular work, live on less money than others who don't have a job in the first place. And who don't want one, either. Unemployed people, who are not working at all, are spoiled by the government in multiple ways. They're released from all kinds of duties and also get all kinds of benefits from the government, too. Certain bills are paid by the state. Schooling, studies, colleges are paid for them. Such benefits are not provided for the ones who are employed or self-employed. And on top of it, the government charges the working class in every possible way, so they have expenses which others have not, who rely on the system already, claiming the doll.

The college where I study and that I can pay for by working almost seven days a week, is also attended by some people who are not working for whatever reason since quite a while. So the government has a program 'to integrate people back into the work market', that says: When someone hasn't been working for a certain period of time he gets some kind of education for free. Paid by the system. Paid by the tax payer. Paid by the people who are working every day. The workless people in my college get so many classes for free, that are part of the educational program that they are on, I could never ever afford myself, not even if I would work additional night shifts. The education they'll get when they leave will extend mine multiple times.

The thing is, that these often don't even *want* what is given to them for free. They cannot value what comes with no effort. They just don't care. In reality that means: They only show up in class once in a while, sometimes only in the afternoon because they needed to sleep in! And I've worked every day to pay for the education I chose out of own initiative. The government invests so much money in people who are unmotivated - they are even sent to private universities - while people like me who are highly motivated get no support.

I know fathers of families, where no one is having a job, and they can't afford to take the jobs offered to them because they would end up with much *less* money than they have, living on the states doll.

Our system is sick!

Of course, there are always some people with personal destinies who are hit hard by their situation. That is especially for people who are alone, or even worse: Who are alone with a child. I personally know some of these cases and know that they do have to struggle. But they are the exceptions. Life is made pretty complicated for them. To be a mother, especially a single mother, is not very appreciated by the government.

But most of those people spend a lot of their time figuring out what kind of benefits they are entitled to get. This is how they make the state finance luxuries such as TV's, mobile phones, washing machines. This way, some have a lifestyle a normal, working person with an average income dreams about. Some absolutely enjoy getting payed for doing nothing, without bad feelings at all. And the sad reality is: They all do *get* payed!

Of course, everyone should have enough support to survive. But in Germany the system is so surreal that people hoarding luxuries whenever they get a chance to, having others paying for it.

Many of the families who are living on the state doll and whom I see every Saturday at the Potsdamer Table in Teltow, are coming in cars, some in small pickups, to pick up their groceries which they are getting for free, because of their so called 'social passes'. I can't afford a car and have to not only pay my college fees by myself but also, of course, for my food, too. In the end, I'm having much less than most of the people who I serve and whose bags and boxes I pack, Saturday after Saturday. They are not suffering hunger. On the opposite. Many of them are overweight.

But wealth alone, that the poorest German lives in compared to the poverty that destines people to die on hunger, obviously doesn't bring fulfillment at all. Even *I* am not happy though. So `being happy` *has* to do something with a certain kind of mind-set, maybe even heart-set, that causes a person to be in a state of happiness or sadness.

The misery of India paints such a dramatic contrast to my own life, that I'm becoming more humble every day I spend here. Satisfied. Happier. Not because the circumstances around me make me happier, but because I'm becoming aware of what is given to me. I'm realizing in what kind of luxury I'm living in, in what kind of richness I have always lived in and that

I'm allowed to live in today. How fortunate am I! How thankful can I be for the life that is given to me!

It's only a few days back when I have not even dared to believe that I would be able to find such feelings in the depth of my soul. But I'm becoming aware of myself and this kind of awareness frees me from the things I suffered from for who knows how long. Maybe my soul suffers the same pain for hundreds, for thousands of years already, from which it can only be healed through exactly the kind of consciousness that opens up for me right here; and that naturally comes to me by doing exactly as I'm told by the scriptures, just following the instructions of the Palm Leafs.

26

I take off my shoes in front of the entrance. This time there are hardly any other pairs.

I'm walking through the gate. A priest comes in my direction and says some incomprehensible words. I turn around and look at Raj who stays outside the gate, waiting. He doesn't wait a second to take off his shoes and to also enter the temple site to come to us.

The temple is just being closed. Raj is talking to the priest for a while and explains to him why we are here. I'm staying right beside them and listen to the sound of the Tamil language that I think is very soothing to listen to. Raj must be telling him about the Palm Leaf Library. He must be telling him that I'm send by the library to visit exactly this special temple and to receive a blessing, because when Raj is done talking, the priest indicates me to come with him. Raj accompanies me, being right by my side.

The gates to the site are being closed anyway. We are all by ourselves in the temple now. The priest relights a candle and takes his tray, similar to the one I have seen in the temple in Madras.

To be send by the library seems to have its very own meaning that everything bows to. The priest paints a line on my forehead with red color, holds the tray with the burning candle in front of me and wants to start talking. Raj and he are exchanging a quick view. My so faithful companion is nodding; that means that he will be translating.

The priest looks at me and says:

"Just trust that at every given point in your life the right things are happening. Be aware that a human being carries everything inside that is needed to live in peace and harmony with the world and everything around. And that destiny will lead our souls home safely.

It is the human craving, the desire and the wish for short-term-pleasures and unnecessary possessions, that causes the drama of mankind and their fights in life.

The reality you created is only the mirror of your soul. Every thoughts and every feeling inside of you strives to the outside, strives to materializes. Your life is what *you* are, and things appear within your consciousness as for what you are able to identify them.

We have responsibility for our body, because it serves the soul as its vehicle. The soul reveals its brightest light through the love towards all beings. This kind of love is the gift that is given to all of us.

Don't let yourself get blinded by the material wealth around you but, on the other side: Don't be careless with the things that are given to you plentifully. Distinguish carefully between what you have and what you are. This is where the healing process of your soul begins. Remember, that every form of self-centeredness goes against the laws of togetherness. Follow your instincts and trust in who you are. This is how you will get in touch with the inner spirit of yourself and all things.

Don't compromise yourself and know, that we are part of something greater than we are, of something that breathes us and guides our lives. Train the visionary ability of your spirit and focus on a higher goal. The key to your souls mission in the earthly spheres lays in what you can imagine, and that become. Become what you see in your deepest dreams and believe in your ability to live your visions. Believe is a powerful force.

Your pictures are given to you from the spheres between all worlds, from Nirvana, from nothingness, from where everything comes from and from where everything goes back to.

Be careful towards and listen to the sensible and soft impulses given to you by your soul, and be real. Remain real and be who you are destined to be. Recognize the oneness of all life so that way the barricades, that hinder your mental development, will vanish. This is the secret of the mystic world.

A human being achieves awareness through the identification with what it loves. Selfless service and the surrendering of your egoistic personality are the ways to make the soul receptive for more sensitive vibrations; and the soul finds its expression through consideration for others and through the love to every part of God's Creation.

The soul incarnates in a physical body but it *is* not the body that is given to you. You are the perceiving consciousness between your soul and your personality.

The confusion between 'being' and 'having' leads to the attachment to matter that causes karma. Our bodies are the vehicles that are given to us so the soul can express itself.

Life is not about hoarding possessions. Life is about understanding, that only love to all living things can bring salvation. Love doesn't ask for worldly rewards and it doesn't need an immediate response. It holds satisfaction right from the moment you open your heart and allow it to flow through you. Acknowledge the responsibility you have for the way you choose, because this is the responsibility you have for life and the world.

In the whole world and in the entire solar system, everything is an impression of the *one* life, that appears in all kinds of different forms and which causes them to be. We are all different expressions of the one, great wholeness and karma is always configured accordingly to the development of each individuals soul. To hold on to things and times feeds egoism, inflexibility and the lack of the ability to let go. This is what causes sorrow. The soul cries thousand of tears when one works against the process of time and tries to hold on, while destiny already opens new chances and wants to show new paths.

One goes from life to life until he realizes the worthlessness of all worldly gratification. Only through the humble service on others and through modesty we will become able to really love.

Your destiny shows you the way that wants to lead you to enlightenment. Trust in your mental guidance and in the higher will, that is always born out of love and that will always flow back into it. Put your personal will under the higher principle of all-encompassing love, so your self can be used for heavenly manifestations.

It is our job to rise to a greater wholeness and to do service to the world. This is when compassion becomes the goal of life, and the sense of your life will be revealed. Realize and to understand all this is what we call the 'grace of God'. But this kind of graciousness can only come upon you when you don't take yourself too seriously. Step out of your way. Let go of your personal desires. Instead, train yourself in devotion to the highest of all achievements: To the love towards every living creature. Understand the laws of creation and take full responsibility for your karma.

Trust the laws of time and space, because they are the prevailing conditions of our existence. Focus your thoughts on the ideal of true humanity, now and instantly.

And remember, that your earlier incarnations also hold their rewards for you. They are presents to us people on the pathways of our lives. Keep that in mind and be thankful.

Your loneliness is only a way on which destiny wants to lead you to yourself. Don't hold on to something that is not there anymore. Free yourself from your emotional dependencies and understand, that all materialization has no meaning anymore as soon as the inner light of the soul has revealed itself to you. God is nothing else but pure love and his home is right within us.

Decide which path you truly want to take. Do you want to walk in the darkness of selfishness or do you want to walk in the light of brotherly love? It is your choice. Whatever you want to orientate your life on is your decision. Rebirth and karma is about nothing else but this. We all have to pass certain initiations in our life. But salvation can only be found through embracing our karma and within the acceptance of the destiny that is given to us.

Self-recognition is the way how to bring out your ability to really love. Go after what you love full-heartedly and do what you feel you are here for. Trust in what you love, because love is God and God is eternity. Identify yourself with the love inside of you, because love alone is the purpose for the entire material kingdom to exist. Let go and make the decision to accept your destiny.

Our ability to understand is the mediator between different realities. Not only between the reality of different people or between the realities of different lives, but also between your personal awareness and infinity, that opens up inside of you.

Make a pact with yourself and give yourself the holy promise to be thankful and to live in love, in good and in bad times. Don't let the worldly matters deceive you. Don't follow your desires blindly. Know that the struggle of your life can only be won through dedication to a higher goal.

Remember the source of your being and use the potential that is given to you. Be aware of yourself and don't mistake time for eternity. Because the road of your life is eventually going to take you to your own death. Every way possible leads to your end. Remember that well and decide wise what you want to use your lifetime for and how you want to spend it. All longings find their fulfillment through the devotion to the all-encompassing love, that lives within each of us and from which we are all a part of. I wish you the best of luck possible, much love and deep peace on your way, whichever is destined for you. And don't forget that one day our souls will be going back to our eternal home, and there *is* this eternal home that is waiting for us."

27

Just as Raj finished saying the last word the priest is looking straight into my eyes. I m looking back. His eyes are clear and full of sympathy. Full of fulfillment. I don't see any longing for another world. I see peace. I see a person who has found what I'm looking for: A treasure, that can never ever be taken away. The meeting with him will change my life. He knows that.

I say goodbye and thank him with a deep bow. Raj as well. Nobody says a word. The gate is reopened and we are leaving the site.

There is no one sitting in front of the temple anymore. It is early afternoon and the sun is burning. We are driving back to the hotel where I'm dropped off, asking for a day off alone.

I have no idea what kind of impact all these experiences will have on my life. But I know that they're changing something inside of me. And that's why I'm sure that all this will change the life I have, or can I already say: The life I *had*?

Every experience, every single thing that happens, is indeed a valuable gain, the moment one is full of trust that our souls will be lead home matured in any case. This way it's impossible to lose. It's just to learn; to see more than we've seen, to experience more than we've already experienced. The cause of our destiny may be laying somewhere deep within our karma and the different emotions that we go through during a lifetime may be only different facets of the variety of Gods creations.

' … a human being achieves awareness through the identification with what he loves ..'.

Identifying with what? I don't have no pictures. When these pictures do exist, why can't I see them? When our visions and our phantasies are the keys to our souls mission, what is mine all about then? I stopped receiving visions a long time ago. There are no pictures anymore. Where are my pictures and visions? And where is my love, or whatever I can identify with? What is between me and them that blocks my vision, that blinds me and lets me walk alone through darkness?

My selfishness? My egoism? My blindness? My self-pity? My mind, which is only focused on my personal needs and which can impossibly see anything other than myself? Or anything that is needed in this world? Anything the soul needs?

28

The next day I'm all by myself, enjoying the sun and the warm weather, the healthy green of the palm trees and the beauty of the hotel park. I sleep in and leave my room around 11 am. It is early December and warm. I'm walking the little walkway, laid out with stoned tiles, to the lobby, sit down in one of the fauteuils, completely surrounded by this beautiful kind of peace. This wonderful, redeeming peace, that has, unnoticed, already started to take over.

I'm already sitting here for 30 minutes when the waiter comes and asks what I wish. I look up to him. The inner stillness remains. Suddenly I understand the essence of the slow motion everything happens in here. A smile rushes through my face which he returns silently.

"A water and a tea, please", I'm saying quietly.

He nods without taking his eyes away from me, smiles, turns around and leaves.

Even if it would take the next three weeks until the tea will be here: I'm fine with it. Time doesn't matter anymore. Maybe time never really mattered for these people and they can't understand why we rush through our days, why we are constantly in a hurry and why we are giving so much meaning to the things we do, so that the most important and most valuable thing that can be given to us has to get lost eventually: Peace.

How many banal things do I pay attention to! How important do I take myself! Me and my feelings, which get entangled in all kinds of stuff that has no deeper meaning and future. And I wonder why I find myself feeling empty after all.

But I do know that there is this point when pain becomes too massive to handle, so people turn away from their feelings and bottle them up somewhere. That's exactly what I did myself. Even though it blocks the insight into deeper levels of understanding, it also keeps this pain locked away so one doesn`t have to feel. Even though we all know that the pain lurks deep inside, waiting for its turn to come.

Superficial pleasures are just another way for the mind to get distracted. Even if we steal the message, brought to us through the pain, away from ourselves by pushing the pain away instead of going through it and listen to what it has to say, it doesn't matter. This price is easily and often paid. I have paid this price easily and for a long time.

Front: Restaurant, Back: Lobby

Lobby of the Green Madows Hotel Resort

My busyness carried me over the time of inner loneliness, but it still was an escape and no solution. I can feel, right here, right now, embedded in this Indian, all-compassing stillness, what I have taken away from me and was running after the same time: Peace. Inner peace. The entire time. All these endless months.

Again and again I allowed my memories to pull me back into my past. I have blocked my vision and have lost the sensibility for myself. I used all my strength to fight my destiny. I prayed, pleaded, cried not to fall into my pain and become its creature. I went all the way to India to find answers and was so afraid not to find anything. That nothing is gonna change. That I'm too blind to see.

But I have found. My fear is gone. I recovered because I did let go. Even though my pain did not just vanish, but it got relativised by what I've seen. I have seen so much sorrow within such a short time period that I happily take the share of sorrow that is given to me. Because I know, compared to others, it is nothing.

My life seems to be over in a weird kind of way I can't really explain. Time stands still, only shadows are moving in the fog. The world I came from doesn't exist anymore. I let things be and wait. I'm Just waiting. There is nothing else I can do anyway because I've ordered a water and a tea and even after half a century they're not here. They probably have to appear out of the depth of nirvana and materialize before they can be served.

In the end I will always remain the same person, no matter what'll happen. And maybe all this time I distracted myself from my own grief wasn't just a form of denial but also opened up another part of me.

Time goes on and my journey through time and space as well. The world will always be the same, only my inner conception will change.

The century that it takes until my order finally arrives I hardly realize. The last time I sat here and waited seemed to be longer.

I turn around to the reception desk. There are the receptionist and the waiter. Both are smiling. And shaking their heads.

29

Last thing I'm told to do, takes me right in to the city. It is written that I shall feed the homeless living on the streets. I'm telling Raj all about it and he recommends to just buy a big sack full of bread and to offer it somewhere right on the sidewalks. We're driving to a quieter part of Chennai which doesn't mean it is quiet in the sense of being still; but it is a little further outside, not in the middle of town. The final destination is a church, build right on the ocean.

It is late noon when we reach the church. The building is white and pompous. It stands out clearly from the street-view of Madras.

The sun burns high in the cloudless sky and the air never moved yet. Just the normal, everyday weather. In front of the entrance, that leads into the area to the church, people are sitting on the hot ground right in the pure sun, meditating. They are just sitting motionless by the fence, their eyes closed, their legs crossed. None of them moves as I walk by.

The stoned pavement of the church areal is made out of noble marble, black and white, laid out in different patterns and designs. I go inside the church. The building is bright and invitingly, the view at the ocean wonderful. The difference between rich and poor can't be overseen. Nevertheless, peace reigns the atmosphere wherever I am. This place makes no exception.

The church is a 'Saint Mary's Church'. Everywhere are statues of Mary and pictures of the holy mother adorns the walls. Instead of a Jesus cross over the alter I can see a big figure of the holy mother: Thy holiness with the child on her arm. It is the first time that I'm in a church that is not built to cherish Jesus Christ and has a cross as the central point but a female holiness. Is there something like that in Germany? Saint Mary's Churches? Maybe in southern Germany but probably not in the Brandenburg area, and if there are, than only in a very few places. I can't remember to have ever seen a single one. No surprise in a country where femininity is mostly suppressed.

In India, on the contrary, femininity is openly *ex*pressed. The women are beautiful, the way they dress is amazing, their long, full hair they show, the long, wide dresses they wear, are stunning. Plus there are so many religions living beside each other, that is seems that one can find just everything existing in form of religion and believe today.

Raj is waiting by the car. He opens the door as he sees me coming and grabs the big, blue plastic sack with bread. It is fresh bread but nothing else but bread, without anything. Raj reassures me that this is the most sensible thing to do and I'm following his advice.

111

I hardly opened the sack on the sidewalk besides the church and signify that I will hand out the bread when, immediately, all the people who were just meditating, sitting on the ground, are jumping to their feed. Within seconds I'm surrounded with humans, ripping the bread out of my hands. They're coming from all directions. It doesn't take a minute and the sack is empty.

The people who were sitting in front of the church were not meditating. They are also starving people, just like the ones in the orphanage, the beggars on the streets, the people on the beach. Now, as they are staying right in front of me, I can see how meager and weak they truly are. They sit there, accepting their destiny, without intervening, waiting for their death. I must be like a revelation for them. They are basically tearing the bread out of my fingers as if there was no tomorrow. And maybe there isn't, for them.

They also bless me, in tears, just like the women from the orphanage. The pictures in my head are still wide awake and clear. I can see the same thankfulness, the same felicity I already recognized in the eyes of the old ladies. They are blissful for what they are given to. They are deeply thankful; able to be thankful. God knows why, but I don't have that ability towards my own life and I'm ashamed of that, being so close to poverty, starvation and death again; having death looking directly at my face, through the eyes of these people.

"Hey, everything Okay? Are you not well?", Raj asked as I sit back in the car.

I'm shaking my head.

"You always look so depressed. May I ask what's going on?"

"By looking at everything I can see and start to understand where I come from and where I'm allowed to live. I'm shaken to see that kind of poverty. But what shatters me even more is the fact, that these people seem to be happier and more fulfilled than I have ever been."

"And that is the reason why you are so quiet and why you want to be alone all the time?"

"Yes, I believe so."

"That's because you people from the western world are eye-people", Raj says.

"Eye-people? What do you mean?" I'm wondering.

His friendly voice:

"Most of all, you believe in what you can see. You say things like: 'I've seen it with my own eyes', taking that for the latest proof that something can be considered as true or not. You are trimmed to have pictures of yourself that you are supposed to become. You associate 'good' with 'good-looking'. Your goals are things like the ideal weight or the ideal face, but the truth is, that those kind of ideals are the scourge for mankind, who declare such outwardnesess to the last and most important instance. Your valuations are orientated on the visible surface. And they are falling apart as soon as invisible things like trust or faith come in to the picture. That's where the fundament of your life suddenly starts trembling."

We look at each other for few moments, silently.

"It's so obvious", he continues. "See, I'm a tour-guide and I had many Germans in my car throughout the time. Alexander procures the connections. And, again and again, I see the same misery. The one on the streets is bad, but I *know* their believe system and that's why I know how these people outside there feel.

113

And if you ask me: The misery I sometimes drive through Chennai on my back seat, is worse. Because you westeners have nothing. You only have things which you can see and touch and that is what you put your focus on, if not your entire life. And on top of that, you can't even realize and see the value of what you own. That is very poor, if you ask me. And it is even poorer when the invisible things are missing. And they *are* missing, that's not hard to tell."

Meanwhile he turned in front on the passengers seat and looks at me through the rear-view mirror.

"You probably do have whatever kind of pictures in your mind, too, that you run after, don't you? Something that you want to be or that you want to become, right?"

"No."

"But you would like to have some", he, smiling.

I nod:

"But the priest in the temple was talking about pictures, too. Didn't he say that our souls mission lies within what we can imagine? And that we should become what we visualize in our deepest dreams? And that we are meant to live the visions that are given to us?"

"That is true. But he also said that you should be aware of the difference between 'having' and 'being'. This is not about visualizing what you will *have* one day. Job and career, that's a part of it. You *have* a job, you *have* a career, but that is not what you *are*. He meant, that you should get aware of what you want to be, *inside*. What kind of person do you want to be? Do you want to be loving or not loving? Gracious or judgmental? Do you want to bless or do you want to comdemn? Those are 'the pictures given to you from the spheres between the worlds'. Ask yourself: What kind of human being do I want to be and 'that become'. That's what he meant. Because the highest, that a human being can achieve during a lifetime, is to become humane. And if God could become humane, than surely human beings can become humane, too.

Most of the things in life remain invisible, you know? If we could only detect what we can see, we would soon be living archives. Somewhen, we will be libraries ourselves, we go in to and search for certain pictures. And if we can't find them, if we can't memorize every single one of them, than you 'look old'. That's how you say it, no?"

I'm nodding.

"But the thing is: The past doesn't matter. The future doesn't matter, because we cannot look into tomorrows land. No one can. Not even the people out there can. Neither can I. They know it. I know it, too. Fear only exists because one is uncertain of what there is to come. To fear the future is only caused by the fact that we can't foresee. But it is not for us to foresee. And that's why it doesn't make sense to have goals you don't know and you can't see anyway.

Our strength, the strength of the Indian people, the spiritual people, is the ability to become familiar with the unknown. We count on the invisible things such as hope, love, grace, humanity, Mahatma Gandhi, Mother Theresa, you understand?"

"Yes", me, quietly, more to myself than to him, "I believe I do".

"All this here is not about *having* something. And it is not about getting certain goods or running after whatever kind of vision. It is about *being* something, right now, right in this moment. It's not about having a certain car or whatever, this is about developing full trust in the always unknown, about trusting life, about believing that everything has its own sense, no matter if we are able to understand it fully or not.

This is why you are suffering so much. You are wondering all the time what you are supposed to do, what you're supposed to become and how everything is going to be. But that's not important. *It doesn't matter*. These things are not for us to know. I can only repeat myself: We can only *be* right in the moment and find fulfillment within hope and within the deepest trust that everything, really everything, has its own sense. Nature doesn't create anything useless or senseless. Everything in this world is here for a reason. And if you want to go even further: Be thankful for the life and the destiny that you are meant to have, because it is the only thing that is really yours. You don't have anymore than that. So, that's why: Take it as what it is because it is the only present that will ever be given to you. And if *you* don't *accept* it, if you can't appreciate it, if you can't be thankful at all, than you will never understand and know the message it holds."

My view disengages from his deep, brown eyes and swifts out of the window to the people starving on the sidewalk, who are already sitting again by the fence, in meditation pose, their legs crossed.

"And it is possible that they are happier than you are", Raj, who followed my view.

"Because they know that their life has a sense. That everything that happens has its sense. And they're living within this deep trust, this deep certainty, that their destiny is meant to be exactly what it is. Everything is right. The experience their soul is going through is, now, meant to be made. Maybe their spirit is even further developed than ours, because it says in the Indian philosophy, that the last life, that one will have on this planet, is a life with no possessions and in service of the soul.

They have blessed you. That's a big thing. Not everybody is doing that. And when these people ever had a job, than they most likely were servants. Also possible that they never had a job and that they are living on charity ever since they were born. In full trust that some kind of higher system, higher being, higher whatever, is going to take care of them. Exactly that higher whatever that gave life to them in the first place. And in the end of all times, the greatest light is waiting for them, Nirvana, and everything they have to do here and now, is to take their present, to accept their share, to be thankful and wait. Everything will, sooner or later, reveal its sense, you know?"

"Ja, I think I do … well … I hope".

"You hope! That's something!"

He smiles.

I'm smiling back.

"Don't get me wrong. I'm not saying you should throw everything away, give everything you have to someone else, live in poverty and be happy. That's not the way. If this experience was meant for you to have, you would surely have it. But your life is not that way, your life is in Germany, in Teltow, right?"

"Right." Teltow and Germany seem to be an eternity away, just as if they would be on some other planet, or be parts of another universe.

"Accept it. Stop asking questions to yourself. Stop searching. Everything is here. Allow yourself and your mind to rest once in a while and stop thinking all the time. You can only hear the message your life has for you when you are quiet. When your mind is still. Your *will* blocks your vision."

"What do you mean?"

"If someone is always searching, it easily happens that he can only see what he is searching for. He has this one goal, he only sees this one goal, he is possessed by this goal and his eyes are blended. He cannot give himself into anything else at that point.

A search is always bonded to a goal. The one cannot exist without the other. But to *find*, means: To be free. To be unattached. To be open. To absorb life and to let it flow through you. That's why: Don't search! You can't find when you're searching. You will only find when you let go. This way you are giving your life and your destiny the chance to find *you*."

I'm smiling at him.

"How long are you gonna be here, by the way?", he asks.

"Three more days."

"Any plans?"

"Back to the library, having the last chapter read."

"Nothing else?"

"Nothing else."

"Okay. I'll hijack you tomorrow for a day."

"Where do you wanna take me?", I'm curious.

"Let me surprise you."

30

Early morning the next day. We're leaving the city, driving through the country side. There are palm trees all over and nature looks mostly untouched.

On the way, we see a cow cart which is used for transport; a horse cart. A very few people by walk. There is hardly traffic on the streets. For long parts of the way we're the only vehicle.

It's never boring in India although we're driving around for hours. In Germany I feel miserable sitting in a car over a long period of time; worse, even, when the sun is shining and the weather is beautiful outside. But here it's different. Here reigns a strange even-minded atmosphere. This sort of stillness. Peace. Everywhere. Even in the car. And the exotic landscape, the nature of the people, the fascinating culture which is to see behind the car class windows are casting their spell over me, every day anew.

We reach a village. Behind it is a neat, beautiful designed city.

"Where are we?", I'm asking.

"Auroville", Raj sais.

"A village?"

"A universal city."

It is green everywhere. Not only the sparsely green of the scanty Fields and meadows of Brandenburg, that have to fight dryness every summer and frost every winter, but the full green and marvelous plants, which leafs are fed by the high humidity throughout the entire year, without disruption. There are plants that have never seen the winters freeze. They have never seen dryness.

We're entering through the main gate and walk on

solid walkways to the main house. The main house in an ashram, originally a prayer house. Around the prayer house there are different zones. One where people live; one where people meditate; one where the different cultures of the world are presented and their history is being told. All that, surrounded by a so called 'green belt'. That is a huge park where all the areas of this city are in.

We're going into the ashram. There is some kind of reception. Books and brochures are lying around. I take one and read:

"Auroville belongs to nobody in particular. Auroville belongs to humanity as a whole. But to live in Auroville, one must be a willing servant of the Divine Consciousness."

"So, a universal city", I'm saying very quietly to Raj.

He nods.

"Who created it?" I wonder.

A woman who is staying behind the desk and obviously heard me, answers:

"Sri Aurobindo had the vision of how living together can work for all people on a universal level. The Mother joined him and put his vision into practice. The concept was than introduced to the UNO, than supported by the UNESCO. 1968 it was inducted by the Indian president to the world. 124 Nations were present. All of them represented themselves. This way they symbolized that this city is 'planetary property'. Every Nation brought earth from their home country. In the center of the city there is a urn of white marble. This is where every nation put the earth in that they've brought. The day of the opening ceremony it got sealed and officially given to the city."

"What a wonderful thought", I'm saying, "but how

did they got this idea?"

"Sri Aurobindo and The Mother wanted to create a basic fundament for a new life structure, that makes it possible for every human being to develop their very own, personal spirituality. Because they knew that mankind only is a certain state within the eternal souls evolution, but not the end. They also knew that living together in the future will only be possible through love and acceptance. Without peace and without love for our neighbors, no future can be possible in the long run. Because we humans will face problems before long which we can only solve together. Overpopulation. Climate change. Scarcity of raw materials. Without mental development we won't be able to handle them. Auroville is supposed to be an example for a possible change."

"What do you mean: Mankind is only a 'state' in evolution?"

"We haven't always been humans and we won't remain humans forever. The next state will be, that life becomes more and more spiritual. Enlightenment. Call it whatever you want to call it. Our bodies will not always be what they are today. Neither will the world always be what it is today."

I'm looking at her. Her eyes are dark, just as dark as Raj's eyes, her view is strong.

"Every piece of mater will pass", she speaks, "it is the spirit that will live on. That's why it makes sense to not focus too much on the material side of life."

My view is sliding back from her to the brochure in my hands. 'Don't collect your treasures here on earth but collect your treasures where nothing and no one can destroy them. Because where your treasure is, is your heart also'.

Isn't this a Gospel of Mathew? I´m looking at her.

"Matter cannot bring fulfillment. It is not made to bring fulfillment. It is not meant to bring fullfillment to us", she says.

I know exactly what you mean.

"But that doesn't mean that you shouldn't enjoy the beauty of this world. We live on one of the most beautiful and greatest planets in the solar system, maybe even *the* greatest. The earth is a miracle. And we are invited to be its guests. We are allowed to live here and we have responsibility for it. It is important to be aware of that. To be aware of the fact that life changes and forms itself new all the time. So our consciousness defines itself new all the time, too, according to that. It is in constant development. We gain more and more awareness. That is the evolution of the mind, of the spirit. Life is awareness. Nothing else. And your life will format itself according to what you are aware of, according to what you believe."

Raj:

"Do you remember what the priest said? Dreams? Pictures? Goals? Coffee?"

"Coffee?", the young lady asks surprised.

"Coffee?", I'm also asking.

"Coffee?", Raj asks, looks at us and smiles.

"Okay", me, smiling back.

"Down the hallway, through the park, at the end of the walkway take a right. There you can get one. Enjoy", the lady waves us good bye.

"Thank you", we say simultaneously.

The park is absolutely fantastic. The little coffee shop, too. We're sitting outside, under some kind of roof that is framed with all kinds of ornamented stones.

"What are you dreaming about?", Raj asks

unexpected.

"I'm dreaming about a life in peace. About freedom. A life in spiritual freedom. For everyone. Not only for me. But for me as well of course", I'm laughing. He laughs, too. "Being detached from all the things I feel so trapped in. Being free. I wish for harmony and peace."

For a second, astonishment gets a hold of my feelings. Can this be true? Did I just articulate a dream? It shines like a bright light into the darkness of my mind: I have a dream!

"That is a fantastic dream", Raj replies. "Why don't you just live in spiritual freedom? It's only up to you, right? You just have to do it, though. Peace, then, comes all by itself", he leans back in his chair and drags on his cigarette.

"There are so many good thoughts are given to me in this country", the words just flow out of my mouth. "My life just gets so enlightened through all these experiences I'm allowed to make, and my horizon widens. I just realize how much I have been focusing on myself all this time, all these years. How my life circled only around my personal needs all together. How egoistic I am! How naive! Naive to believe that the world I'm living in really is everything."

Raj is nodding silently:

"One thing you can already thank the Rishis and the Palm Leaf Libraries for is, that they called you, that they made you leave your life and come to India.

"Ja, I agree."

I'm thinking back to the libraries and the leafs that I've almost already forgotten. The Nadi-Reader, the old, knotted Sanskrit, the translator. 'Don't make any plans for India, because India has plans for you'. How true.

31

Next morning. We're going back to the library. All I was asked to do is done. Money for charity I will leave right here as well as a fee for the Nadi-Reader and the translator.

As we reach the library I get out of the car and go straight into the building. The man behind the desk, right by the entrance, knows exactly who I am and just nods as I walk by. I don't know why but him being there makes me stop, even though he didn't mean to stop me or say anything. I turn around and go back outside.

It takes quite a while until a young man comes to the little waiting area. I've seen him a few times before. He takes me to the prayer room on the ground floor where I left my finger print when I first came here. The altar is decorated, inscents are burning. I'm instructed to put the donations on the altar. This way they get blessed. I'm taking an ornamented envelope out of my bag I found a few days ago in one of the beautiful small shops alongside Madras' streets. That's where I keep the money in. I put it down. Than the man has me perform certain prayers and rituals.

If he's a priest or not, I can't tell. Because everyone has lines and/or dots drawn on their forehead. All of them are wearing the same clothes: Long garments; so it is impossible for me to tell the difference between a priest and an ordinary person. All of them could be priests in my eyes. Everyone seems to be similarly spiritual, too, and all of them are obviously doing their prayer rituals every day. So, it doesn't really make a difference though if someones official profession is being a priest or not.

The man indicates me to go down on my knees and to touch the floor with my forehead. Holy chants are recited, sounding exactly like the ones I've heard in the temple days ago. I knee a few minutes on the floor until the priest gives me a sign. I'm getting up and wait for a few moments, my hands folded, until he passes a tray to me which ritual I already know. Same procedure it seems, because on the tray are powders and a candle. I paint with each powder, white and red, a line on my forehead, take my hands and go, three times, back and forth between the flame and my third eye. Subsequently I refold my hands and close my eyes for a few moments, just staying there, motionless. As I reopen my eyes, the man who indicated me to do all the rituals, looks right in my face, smiling, approving.

Just as I'm staying there, starring at the statues above the altar, an impulse strikes me and I immediately turn around and look at the door. The translator. He must have just arrived. I'm looking straight in his eyes. I can't say weither I'm happily surprised or if I'm taken aback. The short but intense eye contact, which we hold a few moments longer than necessary, is our greeting. We don't say anything. We don't move.

I have arrived. I instantly remember the inner connection I felt towards him after my deepest life secrets, which only he and I know in all its particularity, got lied out right on the table through him. Now we are facing us again, my ally and I, and I know: For the time I'll be here I won't be alone with myself.

Again, this deep kind of knowledge speaks from his eyes, that he seems to have, concerning my life and that I will get to know in a bit. It is, again, this kind of superiority he expresses, without being arrogant or wicked.

It was him who read to me what I had to do and what now is done. He knew what was waiting for me. He knew what I would see and understand. He knew, from the very beginning, what kind of experiences he sent me through. Of course, these things were written in the Palm Leafs and they are not picked by him personally, but he transmitted them. That way he is bond to my destiny and to everything the five thousand year old Leafs held for me. He became a part of my life and one of the most important persons at the turning point of my understanding about human beings and our world, that now looks all anew to me. He doesn't only look *at* me, he looks right inside me.

He turns around and goes up the stairway to the first floor. I follow him. He doesn't need to tell me that I should. Our silent greeting was enough. It was enough for me to come back to my senses. It was enough for everything possible within human communication.

The Nadi-Reader is already there when we enter the little room in which my reading shall find its end. The tape player is ready to record and the Leafs, holding the last chapters of my reading, are laid out on the table. I sit down, facing the two men. The Nadi-Reader starts chanting the familiar sounds.

The chapter Diksha is being read; the spiritual components of my consciousness, that are supposed to be developed, the 'skills' that are needed for my enlightenment. The chapter is unexpectedly short.

I'm told that, in exchange to the donations I left downstairs, someone will speak prayers for me for the next 120 days. Also I'm told that I have spiritual leaders who lead my way and protect me all the time. When I can accept that there are people who pray for me and that there are beings from higher spheres watching over me I will always be protected, than I will be immune against all kinds of frightening and destructive forces.

The translator goes:

"God will lead your way. You life is configured in a certain way so your soul will rise to its greatest growth. You will never be in the lack of anything anymore. You will never have vital problems anymore as soon as you trust in your higher guidance and also in the fact, that you're always protected, no mysterious forces will trouble you and your dreams anymore. Be aware that you are strong. You have the power and all skills that are necessary to make your visions come true."

He raises his view:

"You did all you were set out to do. You resolved karma and gained wisdom no one will be able to take away from you ever. Your life will be peaceful from now on, when you allow it to be. All the things that are going to happen won't appear as catastrophes anymore. All sorrows that were meant for you to appear will only materialize in a very minimalized form, if they'll take place at all. By fulfilling all duties as you were told to, you regained your ability to happiness and joy."

There, this view. Again.

"You will meet somebody. This person will open a door for you so you can bring to an end what here began. As soon as this circle of experience, taking two to three years, is completed, you will have a well-pleased and successful life. You will always be wealthy and a future in peace is ahead of you", he is smiling.

"Now, after all you've done, go to a Saint Mary's church, on a Saturday, and speak prayers there. This is where some important thoughts will be brought to you and that will help you make an important decision."

Some thoughts will be brought to me, that will help me make a decision? I don't say anything and decide to just trust.

The translator is done. That was the last reading. Here, the way that led me into the library, ends.

Of course my life will be peaceful from now on. After all I've seen and experienced, deep discontentment won`t be possible any longer. I'm not able to say anymore that I'm not fortunate, especially not in my home country, a county where hunger and poverty practically don't exist.

I'm doing well, ja, I'm rich and that's what I'll always be. In direct comparison to the lives I have seen and got a bit of an idea of, I will definitely be happy until the end of my days. After all the horrors of starvation and death, which opened up in front of my eyes day after day, nothing that can be happening to me will ever have the power to become a catastrophe anymore. No, I'm safe, protected and don't suffer misery. On the opposite: Real misery has never happened to me until I took this trip. I know that now.

Did I resolve karma? I don't know. But I reached a certain understanding. I understood in what kind of wealth we, in the western world, live in.

Of course, the library-people know where they're sending one to and what sort of experiences they have the searchers to make. And, of course, I'll be able to understand after all, how fortunate I am myself, now, that I've traveled so deep down to the troubled worlds of other humans.

I get up the same moment the translator does. We are facing each other silently. He knew it. He has known it the entire time. And now I know how to interpret the superiority in his eyes that does not carry any sign of pride within, because it is poverty and death on the open streets he knew and knows about and which I was supposed to observe. I was supposed to see all this. It was destined for me to see and to experience it so I can understand who I am and where I come from. So I can understand that Germany is not the end of the world and that the richness of the first world is not universal standard. My problems, which only exist within my mind and not outside of me, are nothing. There is much bigger despair that really *is* despair. All the pain I've ever known just fades away behind this new background picture, that will underline my life from now on.

'... All sorrows, that were meant for you to go through, will only materialize in a very minimalized form, if they'll takes place at all'. Right: My misery is nothing compared to the misery that is possible. And even what I saw is not all there is. But it was enough to change everything.

129

Palm Leaf Library Madras, India 2005

The Palm Leaf Library did its work. It releases me into a new world, because I'm provided with a much better comprehension than the one I had when I came here.

The translator escorts me down the steps, outside, in front of the entrance. Automatically we turn to the little stand on the right. A wink of his hand is the sign for the man behind the counter, that we would like a tea.

Silence. The little tea bowls are put on the wooden desk. Both of us take ours without saying a word. The sweet, warm, milky tea runs down my throat and distracts me for a few seconds.

We are staying together looking down the street for a while. As I'm done I put my bowl back from where I picked it up. It's time for me to go. He knows that. We wait out the moment a little, but then I say good-bye with a deep bow and folded hands, just as it is common in this country. While I turn around he says quietly, almost unnoticeable:

"We will meet again. You'll see."

32

We're driving back to the hotel. My flight is going to leave late tomorrow, back to Berlin through Paris. International flights are leaving at night and my flight is scheduled at 11 pm.

It won't be possible to visit a Saint Mary's church on a Saturday while I'm still in Chennai. Today is Sunday. My flight leaves Monday. And in Berlin? Especially so close to new-year? Is there a Saint Mary's church in

Berlin at all? Potsdam? There is none in Teltow, this I know for sure.

We reach Green Meadows. I remain sitting in the car, looking out of the window. When I, now, get out of the car, it feels like my trip to India is over. I'm not moving. Raj gets out and opens my door:

"So?", he asks, bending down to me.

I'm sighing:

"It's a wired feeling to get out now and to know that it`s all over."

"Nothing is over. Everything just begins. Everything always begins, in every single moment."

"Ja, I'm just saying. It's just strange to leave India. Here it is so peaceful, people are so nice and warm, just like the climate. Germany is cold, in many ways", I'm looking up.

He kneels on the edge of the car:

"I understand what you're saying even though I've never been to Germany. But I've heard a lot", he sighs, too.

"But, you know, everyone who quarrels with his life did not understand the point: That every destiny contains its own experiences; experiences the soul needs to make to gain awareness", he speaks with a voice that carries just as much confidence as wistfulness within.

"Everything has its sense. Every experience is meant to be exactly what it is. Nothing is wrong. Nothing is better or worse than anything else. The destiny you have, the experiences you make, everything is now for you to experience, not later or in another lifetime. Now. Otherwise you wouldn't be where you are and have what you have. So it is senseless to fight with the destiny that is given to you. It is simply a challenge, growth. That's what life is", he smiles.

I'm getting out of the car.

"You did not go your way in vain", he continues.

"Everything in this world has a purpose. Just be real, no matter what you do. This is the key to everything."

I know that we have to say good-bye now. I'm only realizing how close we grew within this short but inspiring two weeks. He is one of the few people who have played an important and decisive part in this. Without Raj, the fulfilling of my tasks and the resolving of my karma wouldn't have been impossible at all. The sense of us meeting has found its fulfilled by doing all I was asked to do. Now it's all done.

"So than", he says, getting back into the car.

"So than", I say and raise my hand for good-bye.

The car starts and slowly takes off. We're looking at each other.

"Thank you", I'm saying very quietly.

He nods. He's heard it.

I watch the car leaving, looking at it until it turns around the corner and drowns in the chaos of the streets of India. My view looses itself for a while within the vast mess of vehicles.

I never saw him ever since.

33

I can't sleep. There are too many things going around my head and I constantly turn from one side to the other. My last night in India. Actually too special to sleep it through. I'm getting up.

As I leave my room, heavy tropical heat strikes me. It is two o'clock in the morning. But the open-air-sauna doesn't care.

The swimming-pool to my right is illuminated from the ground and the light shines through the darkness of the night. I sit down in the grass, looking into the water, into the sky, looking at the trees, which colors change from green during daytime to black during the night.

The sky is clear. I can't see any clouds, just stars. But Madras is too bright for them to really shine. The only thing shining is the pool.

I lay down right where I am. The little hotel resort is quiet. Again I'm the only one in the entire park. Maybe I'm even the only one in the entire hotel? I don't know. From far away I can hear the noisiness of Madras' streets. Honking, Rickshaws, Motorbikes. I close my eyes and breathe in all the sounds, the warmth, the atmosphere with all its stillness that is carries within. I want it to be part of me. I suck this stillness in, to every cell, into every part of my body. It shall settle itself deep within my soul and remain forever. A warm, delightful feeling flows through me before I fall asleep.

In my dreams I can see, again, all humans, all the people of the world. But this time, not as beings levitating through space; this time, we're all standing beside each other in a one, long row. Everybody. The entire human race.

We are all light. We all look the same. We are body-shaped, but we are light.

There is one standing in front of us, facing us. He is some kind of messenger. A messenger from higher spheres as we are all aware of, and he's here to speak to us.

We're all holding each other by the hands. The energy circulates between us, it circulates through us, through each one, up to the end of the line. We're looking at the speaker. For quite a while, there is just unity and peace. We are all paying full attention to the messenger, the angel, the higher light being who looks back at us and finally delivers his message:

"*You are here to shine.*"

34

As I awake, the sun is already up. I'm trying to get up, too. My back hurts. Sleeping on the pure ground is not for me. I get myself up. A person has about 200 bones. At least half of them hurt. In this country, enough people sleep on the blank concreted ground! I absolutely don't get how they manage.

The waiter sees me and looks for a while in my direction. I smile and shake my head. I learned how to do that while staying in this hotel. I had enough opportunities to watch the people working here doing it. Does he think it's common for hotel guests to sleep outside on the ground rather than in their beds? Doesn't matter.

I'm limping to my room. A warm shower for my tortured bones would be a blessing right now, but however pretty and beautiful the resort looks: There is no warm water in the hotel. Whatever is standard in a German hotel, is the luxury of a five star Hotel in India.

The day flights by, without me noticing it really. I'm strolling through the park, deciding to go down to the ocean one more time. The beach is beautiful. No one is here. I sit down in the sand and look over the water.

It's my 12th day in India. It's not even two weeks ago that I've been sitting here. Thinking about it feels as if an entire lifetime lies between now and then. I look inside of me, but can't find any of the heavy feelings I still carried in my soul when I first arrived. This country liberated me. It took my sadness away, made me let go of sadness and despair.

A wave of contentment rushes through me. Stillness comes down on my mind. And peace. This wonderful kind of peace I was longing for so long.

I came here to look for my treasure.

The search was successful.

35

It feels like night time as Alexander Bilson comes to the hotel. It's already getting dark, although it is only somewhen around seven. He knocks on my door, comes in, takes a seat at the little table that stands in a corner of the room and watches me pack.

"Alexander, I feel as if the life I left doesn't exist anymore."

"I know."

"And I have no idea what kind of life is waiting for me when I get back. Somehow everything is so different."

"I know."

"And I can't imagine that anything will still be the same when I get home? And that anything will still be what it was when I left."

"I know", he says repeatedly and smiles this Indian kind of smile that puts a warm veil over my heart, every time.

"What do you mean *you know* I'm asking, stop packing and sit down on the edge of the bed.

"India leaves no one untouched", he starts explaining. "I have known, right when we first met, that the live you had would not be existing anymore when you get back. I'm living in India for thirteen years now. I have never met anyone who came here and whose understanding of life did not change drastically. I assumed that the same thing would happen to you. Your life was over the moment you made the decision to leave Germany. The little bit *I* did to it is nothing compared to what this country has done for you."

We are facing each other for a while, silently.

"The problem is, that we are too attached to matter and that we live against our nature", I then say.

"No, that's not the problem."

"It is not? But that's exactly what the scriptures are talking about, no? And the people here. And the priest in the temple, for example."

"I believe all matter is God-like", Alexander says.

"Ja, nature may be", I'm stating.

"No, I believe everything else also."

I'm still looking at him, now with questions in my eyes, wondering. He recognizes it and explains:

"In the beginning of everything there is always the idea first, right? Your trip to India began with the idea of coming here, with the idea to visit the libraries, long before anything was even put into practice. All you can see and touch started the same way: With an idea. The chair I sit on; the table we eat on. On a certain point of time, someone had the idea of it. And ideas are something you get, you receive. Not something that you make yourself. To put an idea into practice is what we can do, but we can't create the idea itself. It is given to us."

He smiles, leans forward and rests his elbows on his knees:

"And where do they come from? No one knows. Just like no one knows where the universe comes from. A big-bang, sure, but what caused it to happen? No living human being on this planet knows that. So, where do our ideas come from? They come from the same unknown space like the Universe itself; they come from the spheres which have already existed, before anything ever really was. And because we can't look into 'before', how can we look into the moment that caused our ideas? "

I say nothing but wait expectantly how the he'll go on.

"Okay, anyway. On a certain point of time somebody had the idea of a table, right? Then, the idea was put into practice and now we have tables in this world. Have we created the idea of it? No! We only build them in the end, nothing else.

Every piece of matter carries the original idea within. This is why everything, everything you can see and touch, carries a glimpse of this infinite, eternal, Godly light inside. A glimpse of that *something* that has been there before anything came into being and what will be there after all has will long be past. *Something* of what has been there before the universe began and what will be there after it'll come to an end."

138

I slowly stroke with my hand along the edge of the bed.

"This means, even this bed is God-like? The cup I drink my tea out of and the suitcase I'm packing? The clothes I wear, ja, even the thoughts I'm thinking!"

"If you want to look at it this way, yes", he calmly replies and leans back in his chair.

"And the question is not, if nature is God-like, but the question is: What is nature?"

"What is nature", I'm repeating, thoughtless, starring out of the window to my left.

"What *is* nature?" I then ask him directly, not waiting for an answer but keeping on talking:

"Nature is what we call *the Devine* than, right? Does that mean, that everything in this world, everything we do, every idea we have, is natural *and* Devine the same time?"

"Of course", Alexander smiles. "That's probably what the priest meant, too. Allow the intuition to unfold and don't judge. Let go of your personal ideas and follow the inspirations that come to you through your instincts. And they do *come* to you. They always do."

"Do you live that way?" I ask him.

"I suppose I do", he answers. "That's exactly why *I* followed *your* instinct to come to India. I did not put myself in the way, on the opposite: I made the way free for you. That way I try to handle actually everything. It's very easy", he smiles again, my heart immediately warms up a bit.

I get on with packing. After a while he asks:

"What did you believe?"

"What do you mean?" I wonder.

"Well, when you got the idea to come to Madras: What did you believe would happen?"

"I don't know what I've believed. I don't really know what I thought. I don't know. I only know that I was fed up with my life, with all the things my mind got bombarded with all the time; and that I didn't want to go on like that. I prayed that all that would come to an end."

"See, and your prayers were answered. An idea was given to you: To go to the libraries. You followed and put it into practice. I bet your life already felt better and more balanced the moment you decided to follow your idea and not to stay in its way, right?"

I'm thinking back:

"Yes, that is right", I'm just realizing, "right on from the very first moment."

"That's how it is. That's why I follow my intuition and the things that turn up. Living that way makes life a lot easier and most of all: Less stressful instead of intervening all the time. Trying to control life all the time can be very tiring if you ask me."

"You're right!"

"Just let go, accept your life and follow your inspirations. That's all you can do anyway. This way, pressure will be released and misery will end. Your old life is over. That doesn't exist anymore. And your new one will begin the moment you put it into practice."

I pause and sit back down on the edge of the bed.

He nods at me and says:

"From the very beginning, a way back into the way your mind was set before you came and the way you lived, has never existed."

36

"We have another 1 ½ hours until the flight leaves. Do you want to go have something to drink? Maybe a water or a tea?" Alexander asks.

"Are you crazy? 1 ½ hours? Do you really think they can deliver an order in such a `short time`? I don't want to miss my flight", the words just automatically blurting out of my mouth.

He laughs. He knows exactly what I'm talking about.

"Let's rather go early to the airport. I don't really trust traffic", I remark.

"Okay!" he immediately gets up. "And if we do want something and there is still some time left, we'll get a tea somewhere on the streets. Tea is one thing you get everywhere."

"Good idea!"

My suitcase is almost ready. Alexanders driver is waiting outside. All of a sudden everything happens very fast. I hardly know it and I'm already sitting in the back seat of that Indian Ambassador, stuck in traffic in the middle of the chaos of Madras` streets.

Alexander is talking. Telling stories about India, historical backgrounds about all kind of buildings. I'm only paying half my attention to what he sais, instead I sink into all kinds of pictures that arise in my memory. His words are the background sound to my thoughts. They feel like a smooth rain on a warm summer day. Even though every day is a warm summer day in India.

I don't speak much on the way to the airport. My view glides out of the window, over the countless numbers of shops, the masses of people, the traffic, the cows.

It is eight o'clock at night and already dark. The vision of me walking through the streets of India appears again. The picture I had before. The word of the Palm Leaf Reader didn't change a thing about it.

How does one live in this country? How does one adopt to a culture that is so different and other than the own? How can one deal with this language? Would I be lonely, living here as a foreigner? Alone? Isolated? Or would one become alike them? Is that possible? What plans would India have for a person whose way leads him or her far away from home to such a place? What would this land hold for someone from another world?

What India held for me so far was so overwhelming, that it is impossible to assume what these experiences will do to me in the long run. I was too deeply touched by what I was allowed to see, too shocked. My outlook of life got turned upside down, unknown depth of feelings opened up for me. I have seen scenes, strange and unexpected. New worlds have opened up right in front of my eyes and I could look into the abyss of starvation and death. I have seen what poverty means, looked in the eyes of people dying and felt the same time full acceptance of their destiny, without resistance, thankfulness even. I felt gratitude and happiness which were so real, that they touched my heart.

We are stuck in traffic. Of course we are, we're in Madras. Stop and go and wait. Nevertheless we get closer to the airport and reach it two hours later after a way of not even seven miles. It is 10 pm. My flight is leaving shortly after 11. We don't have much time left. Alexander takes my suitcase out of the car, puts it on a trolly the driver got and we rush to the entrance.

"I can't come with you from here on", I hear Alexanders voice from behind. He hands me my suitcase which I take without a word.

"The trolly has to stay here, too."

We take a step aside so we won't be in everybody's way.

I don't know what I'm supposed to say. We're just looking at each other. After a while Alexander points with his head in the direction of security I now have to pass. I turn around, slowly start to walk toward where I have to go and find myself in the middle of a terrible crowd of people, suitcases and bags. Just when I past through security I turn back around, but I can't see no one. Alexander is already gone.

37

I turn around and walk through the long hallways of the airport. I hardly reached my gate when the check-in begins. I'm booked to my seat. It's a window seat. The plane is not as full as it was on the previous flight. The seat beside me remains empty.

While the plane takes off I can see the sparse lights of Madras which start to disappear into the darkness of the night. Somewhere down there is Alexander, Raj, the Palm Leafs. Somewhere there, in the dark of this other world, that gets darker and is further away with every mile we gain in altitude, lay mysticism, secrets and many cows on the open streets. Soon Madras vanishes from my sight.

I'm leaning back. The farewell hurts a little bit, but I know: I will be back, very soon even. That's what my feelings are telling me. Despite of all the translator told me. Even if that's not written. In a strange way I already feel closer to India than I have ever felt to Germany.

Out of the little window of the plane I can see nothing more than darkness. I get with my face to the window as close as I can, take my hands and seal my eyes up against the light inside the plane as good as I possible. Because it is brighter inside than outside and I can hardly see the stars in the clear sky, although I'm closer to them than I have ever been before.

The air plane goes to Germany, but where will I arrive? What will my world look like, now that I know what I know and after I have seen what I saw? Everything will be new. Germany won't be what it used to be when I left. My sight is a bit clearer, my mind a little more open and my soul wider.

It is late. Even though I have not slept much last night I'm not tired. I close my eyes and imagine that the plane will fly forever though the clear night that is so full of stars, and that I would never have to return down to earth. But my story goes on. India's plans for me are not fulfilled yet.

But I feel fulfilled and thankful. What a treasure! A treasure that can never be taken away by no one no more.

38

It is Tuesday, December 8, when the plane lands in Paris, after an eight and a half hour flight. It takes another 1 1/2 hours and I'm back in Berlin Tegel. I leave the plane with a mixture of all kinds of feelings and walk down the halls. I wait for my luggage, take it from the conveyor as it comes and leave the area through an automatic glass door, that is secured by two armed men and which slides open as I get near it. My mother is already waiting for me outside. She welcomes me happily but senses immediately that I don't feel like talking. Mothers do feel such things. She has a sixth sense for how I feel. Even the tone of my voice through the telephone, when I say a simple and short 'hello', makes her recognize the state of my emotional condition.

It is cold and rainy. Fortunately my mother has enough decency not to force a conversation on me on our way home. We don't say anything most of the drive through Berlin.

The following Thursday I'm booked to play the piano at a Christmas party in Teltow. I get there as planned but I'm only physically present. I do play, but my soul and my mind are still somewhere in the streets of Madras. My fingers slide over the keys like remote-controlled. I reel off the usual program that is requested on such kind of occasions, can hear me play from afar and wonder how it is possible that I hit even one single tone right. Because my thoughts are thousands of miles away, somewhere between Palm Leafs, temples and dying people.

I have not fully arrived yet. The impressions of my trip are slowly taking effect on me in all their intensity. Pictures are arising and disappearing. I can't hold a single image in my mind, I can't see no context. I have no idea who I am. I'm in a place I don't belong to anymore. I'm with people I know for such a long time and who have never been as strange to me as they are now.

Time flies. The night is over before I realize it. The next day flies by as well, and soon it is Saturday. Every Saturday I work at the Potsdamer Table. From early morning till late afternoon, pickups come and bring food that is thrown out from supermarkets around.

There is a law in Germany that says, that certain foods are not allowed to remain in the store for more than one week. After a week it *has* to be thrown away, no matter in what condition it is in. This is especially the case for perishable foods like vegetables and fruits. As a matter of fact the Potsdamer Table is almost swamped with all kind of things, even though there is only a small number of supermarkets that are giving their goods away. If all grocery stores would give their stuff to one of the food counters, than the free market would collapse, because we would have so much food to give away for free that we could feed entire cities. Practically no one would have to go shopping anymore. To prevent this from happening, most supermarkets simply trash their stuff.

But even the way it is, we have enough food to feed all the people who come, no matter if they have a social pass - which is actually required to get food for free - or not. We are nine people working there pro bono. All of us are busy from morning to late afternoon, sorting food that is brought in big boxes, completely mixed up. The supermarkets don't make the effort to sort their discarded goods themselves before they put it outside, when the table comes to pick it up.

At about five, the food out-put begins. I find myself between mountains of boxes, each stuffed with the most beautiful things: unspoiled paprika peppers,

146

apples, bananas, fruits of the season, all kinds of salads. Bread and cake in such masses, that we need an extra room where the pallets are piled, up to the ceiling.

Every week there is a long line of people waiting in front of the place. Everyone can pick whatever they like and we are there to pack the groceries in the bags and boxes they bring.

It is not much room on the yard, and the little space is mostly taken by the cars the 'poor' and 'needy' come with, to transport their items. Most of them cannot carry what they take away by walk alone, this is how much they are taking away.

"What's 'dis s'pposed de be?", a voice out of the crowed.

I can see how a man lifts an apple that has a small, brown spot.

"We're gettin pig food, don't ya know?" quacks a woman, who is standing in line, just getting her third box packed.

"Who knows where dis is gonna end one day", sounds a voice behind me. One of our honorarys.

The people who work there are allowed to take whatever they want, officially *after* everyone else is gone. But the reality is, that most of our own people pick the nicest things out of all there is, and that is *before* anyone has even been here. Many of them arrive in the morning the same moment the Table comes and opens the transporter the first time; they usually start packing their own boxes and bags immediately. Picking the nicest and the best, to then hide their stuff back in the kitchen, where no one else is allowed to go. Unofficially of course. Because that is strictly prohibited. But they don't care.

"In what kind a disgraceful circumstances we have 'de live here! Shameful!" I hear another voice from one of the team members.

"Pathetic", another one says.

I don't say anything. The behavior of these people shock me, even though I have known it now for so many months. I can hardly believe that I have worked here for all this time. I keep silent.

At night, after every receiver is served, farmers come to pick up the very rest that is left, taking it for their pigs. They also come with transporters and trailers, taking boxes still full of vegetables and fruits. Even the animals are fed for free with food, starving people in India would dream about.

I lift my view and see people with hardened faces and cold eyes. None of them is under weight. Rather the opposite mostly. And most of them carry the same dissatisfaction inside, demonstrating it, without shame. They seem to be unsatisfied, because they are not aware of the wealth they are living in. In my eyes they are demanding and unthankful. Unthankful for the life that is given to them. Unthankful for the abundance they are living in. Unthankful for the fact, how naturally the German system satisfies their needs.

The term 'needy' and 'poor' loses its meaning the moment I'm watching this scene. I can't see no need anymore. I can't see poverty. I don't understand their discontent, neither their anger. I can't see any deficiency and I can't feel any sympathy for them anymore.

Immediately I let go off what I just held in my hands and take a step back. The take-out is fully going on but the scene seems to be unreal. I'm not a part of it

148

any more. I can't be here any longer. Absolutely impossible.

My hands unbind my apron all by themselves. I cross the yard, go inside, take my handbag, leave the food counter to never went back there again.

39

Nothing in my life is as it used to be. Everything is new and different. Familiar things feel strange to me, the common talk of people around bores me. I want to exchange some thoughts, but with whom? I want to speak with someone, but there is no one who understands.

The days after my arrival I'm alone most of the time. I produce an entire album with piano music within a few weeks, trying to express the deep feelings and all the sensitivity India awoke inside of me. I want to touch, because I'm deeply touched myself. I can't find words which would describe what my trip to this mystic world has done to me. And there seems to be no one who understands anyway. I'm deeply affected and I hope that these feelings will find their resonance in the music I record. The tones are gentle and quiet. They're floating freely through the space of my room. They're so very quiet, just as if it is almost unreal that they even exist. The songs are slow, so slowly like my astonishment that still reigns my soul and disconnects me from the world I used to live in.

In my emails I repeatedly find a message from this unsympathetic man I met in the plane. He already send me a sms to my mobile while I was still in

Madras. I didn't answer. Neither did I answer his first mail he must have written while I was still in India and which I found only after I got back. His second mail comes during the days of my solitariness, when I'm not doing anything else but dreaming and playing music.

He asks me how my trip was. If I liked Chennai and what the Palm Leaf Reader said. I'm kind of impressed by the consistency of this man, whom I repeatedly asked to leave me alone when we first met and whose tries to reach me never got a reply so far. That's why I decide to write to him. I remember that he mentioned that he is originated in Madras. Maybe he is able to understand how I feel.

Nevertheless I keep my reply short and shallow, because I can still sense the repulsive feeling towards him that made me ask him to leave I don't know how many times.

My finger hardly hit the send-button when my phone rings. Sam calls from his office in New York. We're six hours apart. It's early afternoon in NY, early nighttime in Teltow and already dark outside. It is winter. The longest night of the year is just ahead of us. There are candles burning in my apartment; the smooth light is beautiful and I'm alone with my piano.

A pretty loud: "How are you?" echos through the phone, "how was your trip?"

"Impressing", I reply. "Deeply impressing. I can't even tell you how I feel. I just can't put it in words."

"I know", Sam says, his voice calming down a bit, "I know that well. India changes the life of everybody who ever travels to that country. It leaves no one untouched."

"Ja, that's true. Ever since I came back home I feel like a stranger in my own town. Somehow I can't reach nobody anymore. I talk to friends and relatives, but they all seem to be far away, living in another world. None of them can understand me."

"When you make certain experiences others don't have and can't share, then it sometimes pulls you away from relationships. That's the same with everybody. That's why especially those kind of people understand each other and feel the closest, who have been through the same kind of experiences. Mostly anyway. That's the secret of relationships. Now, to know about India and about the conditions people live in, disconnects you from the relationships you had and from people who have never experienced all this. That's very natural."

"Exactly that's how I feel and I feel alone, though. I have no one I can talk to or share my loneliness with."

"So share it with me then. I know it, too. Very well even. When I came to America I've been very alone. I didn't know anybody. Phone calls were too expensive at that time and emails practically didn't exist then. That was loneliness, I can tell you!"

"How is it possible to bring the pictures of the third world and the feeling of personal satisfaction, the common satiety of the first world, together? And how can I be around people, who all don't know the third world and who are so unhappy with all they've got, complaining all the time? Can I live that way? Is that possible or will I feel strange and disconnected in my own home country from now on for all times?"

"You can't do anything about the circumstances around you. You can always only live your own life. As long as you're depending on the comfort and the understanding of your environment, you will suffer as soon as that kind of understanding is not there anymore. You'll be unhappy as soon as the environment you depend on doesn't honor you anymore. That's a modern form of slavery."

I sigh. He's right. I have nothing to reply. I never expected to hear such comforting words from this person. I don't need to explain much. He has the same pictures in his head like I do, he sees the same city in front of his inner eyes, the same places. It's absolutely unnecessary to say much. He knows about the circumstances under which life takes place in India, much better than I do; but even though he does, he seems to be happy!

"You know", he says, "I believe life is all about going your own, individual way. That's how you're fulfilling karma. Let the others be the others. It was destined for you to go to India. Just as it was destined for the relationships to your friends to maybe end now, because your point of view has changed. All this wouldn't happen if it weren't part of the great plan of your soul. Just trust that everything that takes place is right somehow, okay? Just go on doing what you're here for."

Sam's words are touching me. Looking at life from his perspective makes everything look just fine. Of course, nothing of all this wouldn't happen, if it wasn't meant to. That's what the Indian philosophies are describing, very detailed though. This is, what we understand as destiny and what the Indians call 'karma'.

"Who are you?" I'm asking.

"What do you mean? Who am I? Just an ordinary man, one of these boring bankers, why?"

I'm laughing. Sam laughs, too. I hear a laughter that absolutely doesn't fit into the picture I have of this man. So different from his voice. As if it doesn't belong to him. Very high, almost childish.

"I'm the oldest of six siblings and I'm born in Chennai. My family was very poor and India was even poorer back when I grew up than it is today. On my way to school I regularly passed by dying and dead people. That's different today. What you've seen is only a fraction of what I've seen when I was a child. We couldn't even afford the most simple sandals and you saw how much they cost. A few rupees, probably not more than one euro. Back than, they have been even cheaper.

At night we slept on the pure floor, all in one room. Sometimes we put water on the floor and laid down in it, because it was so hot outside. But it didn't help, really.

I always knew: If there is any way in this world that could possibly take me out of this misery, it can only be my education. I cannot remember that I've done anything else in my early years than studying for school. I sacrificed my entire youth for the chance of a better life.

The life I've seen on the streets scared me. This fear is there, until today. It keeps my engine running all the time. And makes me do the things I do. It makes me work as hard as I can, every day. The fear of becoming poor and starve to death sits deep and is always present."

His story relativizes my loneliness to such an extent, that I can't feel it at all while he's speaking.

"There is a system of high quality universities in India. Only the top students of every class have a chance to get admitted. They have to pass a test. Not like in America, where mostly the people with money can attend college. In India the universities cost money, too, but it is not comparable with what they cost in the US or elsewhere.

There are entire stadiums, filled with candidates. 20.000 people applied in Madras alone in my year. 10 got in. I was one of them. I.I.T., that's what these universities are called. I.I.T. saved my life. The long years I spend studying payed off in the end.

As I was done with I.I.T., my father took the money he saved for years and bought me a one-way ticket to America. I was sent away, to a better world. From the third to the first. And because I'm the first born child in my family I knew, that my brothers and sisters would follow my example. That's how it is in Indian families. I had no other choice than to somehow make it through in this new, far away country.

Feelings were nothing we could afford to care about. It didn't matter how I felt. No one asked how I felt anyway. That I was sent away and that I left had nothing to do with idealism. It was the pure instinct of survival that drove our decisions.

When I came to the US, I could not afford an own place so I found a family who let me sleep on their living room couch for very little money.

But I made it. I made it through. I have suffered all these years and put myself through misery. I put myself in the back seat and had practically no personal wishes, no personal life.

Today I'm a banker. I work in New York and just founded my first investment fund with four additional partners. I've worked for every single piece in my life. Nothing was given to me. I'm not born and raised in the first world. But I always tried to make the best out of every situation. Numbers and figures, this is what I do well. That's my metier. I didn't have much choice either anyway. And that's why I don't think about it, I just do it. We can always only make something out of what is given to us. We have to use our talents and make something out of them. That is our task and our duty. It is karma *who* you are and what talents are given to you. Your talents are the gifts given to you that help you to make a life. And by using the talents that are given to you, you're fulfilling your karma. That's why we're here, if you asked me. That's the reason why we are alive after all."

Sam's words are medicine to me. From now on, we're speaking with each other every day. He speaks right from my soul and understands me. He's the only one I feel able to communicate with. The conversations with Sam free me from my loneliness and isolation. He senses that, and feels a bit like my savior which he, may be, somehow is.

With everyday that goes by I can feel that we're getting closer. Within a few weeks he turns out to be the only one I'm talking to at all.

No one understands me anymore except of him. Nobody knows India. None of my friends and relatives have an idea what I mean, when I'm telling all about the depth of human misery I have looked in to. They're nodding and think that my travelogues are 'exciting', but no matter what I say: They remain outsiders and listeners. They are not involved, not like-minded.

There is only one person who understands, and this person is Sam. Only with him I can speak. We are traveling the same inner worlds of experiences and we have one thing in common: We both hold images of the third world, living in the first the same time. Even though America and Germany are far away from each other, the distance we both subjectively feel is infinitesimal small. I'm close to him. Despite of all the miles between us, closer than I am to any other person.

40

Sam insists to see me, but I can't afford nor imagine to take another trip right now. I just got back. Besides, the plan was to get prepared for my exams these days. It's close to Christmas. The days still get shorter and the nights longer. My loneliness grows stronger, the nights grow darker. Just as I can hardly stand it anymore, I'm asking Sam via email what would be if I took into consideration to come see him. Not even a minute after I send the email, my phone rings. I answer and hear Sam saying:

"No problem! I'll send you a ticket and you just come here."

Money is not an issue for Sam. Throughout the years he made so much profit with investments and stocks that he is a multimillionaire. But money is about all he has. He doesn't have anything else than that. He feels very alone, too, and is not always as happy as it seemed when we first talked on the phone.

My trip to the USA is set up. My flight goes through New York to Charlotte, North Carolina. Sam is going to visit his brother, than planned to rent a car, go to

Atlanta to see his sister and fly back to NY where we will celebrate New Year.

December 24. Christmas Eve. I'm at home with my brother. Only he knows about the wired encounter with Sam and that I plan to go meet him. I can hardly remember what Sam looks like. When we first met I didn't really look at him. I know his face only from pictures he send me by mail.

"But what happens if you don't get along and he is not the one you believe he is? Then, all this was only a big bubble and a dead dream. What then?" My brother worries.

My brother gets easily worried. Basically he is constantly worried. Actually, he is worried all the time.

"That wouldn't be the problem", I'm saying. "The problem would be, when exactly the opposite is the case; and my feeling tells me that this relationship is going to happen. What, if we *do* get along and he wants a life with me? What would that mean to me and *my* life? He is a banker with a successful career. Anyhow, on top of that, he just founded an investment fund and is going to build the business branch in India. He is just in the process of moving from the great finance center of America, which is New York, to the one in India, Bombay, the second biggest slum in the world, right after Rio De Janeiro. What then?"

My brothers look tells me that he doesn't believe that this will be the case.

"I don't have a life here anymore, Dan", my voice is low and I look on the floor we're sitting on. "I have no idea what I'm here for. I just don't see no way. There is nothing here for me. And then there is Sam. I was longing, I was praying, to meet *my Sam*, you know? That's what I wished for. I hoped so much that I would meet somebody who would share my life, protect it a bit, maybe even someone who could save it some. It almost looks like my wish became true.

Everything, really everything, is better than a life here. I don't get along here very well, and it is even worse after I came back. In India there are people lying dead on the open streets and here we have problems of the rich and greedy. And everybody here *is* rich compared to each of them and still: There are constant complaints about everything all the time. I can't stand it anymore! I just want to get out of here!"

My brother is still looking at me. He can see in my eyes that I'm already not here anymore, that I'm already gone. What is he supposed to say? He doesn't say anything.

That night we are sitting together for a long time, silently. The next morning, 7 am, my flight leaves from the same airport from where I took off four weeks ago through Paris to Madras. Now the plane takes me to the other side of the world, to America, to my first meeting with a man who is basically a stranger to me and who is the only one able to bring a little light into my life.

41

I have never been in New York before. I only know Iowa from the years 1992 – 93, but I still remember the flair, the atmosphere, the American spirit lying in the air. So I don't feel completely strange as I arrive at John F. Kennedy airport even though I've never been here before.

My connecting flight to Charlotte gets canceled because of the weather, but I have a long and intense discussion with the woman behind the counter until she books me on another flight. I do reach South Carolina the same night.

While I'm talking I can feel how much I must have missed this country, because it seems like a big weight falls off my soul now that I'm back. I left Germany behind. It feels like a huge release after a long endured pressure, even though I can't really tell what this pressure was all about.

It's late at night as I'm waiting in Charlotte for my luggage. It doesn't arrive. I receive Sam with empty hands. I have nothing except of my small handbag. My suitcase is somewhere between the east coast and the southern states.

I'm completely dependent on this unknown man. This situation should remain for the next three years the Palm Leaf Reader already talked about, but which I'm not aware of in this moment at all.

I feel my life is back in its natural flow ever since I left Teltow. All negative feelings have already fallen off of me entirely.

I'm not surprised that I find myself in America soon after the overwhelming experiences I went through in

India. Although I would have never ever dreamed about going in the US so soon.

The Indian culture I'm confronted with through Sam doesn't appear all new to me, nor unknown. It actually feels pretty familiar even though Sam's brother is really weird. Sanjiv is married to an Indian woman from his home town. It was a traditionally arranged marriage. That's what he had requested. The parents picked the wife. Sanjiv and his fiancé have seen each other before the wedding and he agreed to the choice his parents made, but they have not really what we consider as 'know' one another.

"An Indian woman is more appropriate for an Indian man", he explains to me.

Today, a few years later, they're having a one year old son who gets spoiled in any possible way.

It is already after midnight as we get there. The family lives in a typical American house, build out of wood, in white color, very roomy inside. Inside we're entering a big hall. It is the kitchen that grades in the living room. Sanjiv offers us some tea which his wife serves silently on a silver tray. We're staying all together in the kitchen, talking; only his wife doesn't say anything and is waiting for orders when a short, quiet grizzle from the child's room is hearable. Sanjiv throws a view upon her, so cold and relentless that my blood freezes in my veins. She immediately runs - she does not walk - she *runs* to the room and disappears behind the door.

She appears to me shy and insecure, without an own will, without independent power over her own decisions. She is the slave to this man and the mother of his children. That is her life purpose, that is the entire reason for her being, this is what defines her identity. He sees her as his property. This is what his authoritarian behavior reveals. Compromises are not allowed. Discussions do not exist. The only rule her life is controlled by is obedience.

Many Indian women get married very soon, sometimes even before they're fully educated or before they've reached the age of 18. Sam's mother was 15 when she got married to his father. She had children in her life and besides that, there was nothing except of the everyday struggle of a slave.

All these impressions and experiences go past me without getting to me at all. I'm noticing them though, but they're taking place without having an impact on me; they've nothing to do with me at all: Neither the way Sanjiv treats his wife, nor the story of his mother. None of these things refer to me or Sam. I don't even give it a second thought. I absolutely don't see the connection between what I see and hear, to possible expectations Sam might hide towards me. Our case is entirely different. Special. Totally unique. Absolutely out of comparison. I think.

42

I'm fascinated by Sam. During the ride from Charlotte to Atlanta he talks without interruption. He's telling stories from his life:

"I live in Manhattan for many years now. I've worked for Lehman Brothers and Goldman Sachs before I founded the Fond with my partners. I was there when 9/11 happened. I've been in my previous office right across the towers. I've heard the first plane crash into

the building. Everybody in the office was starring out of the window, watching the plane burn, exchanging views. Sms's and emails came in and out like crazy, it was beeping everywhere and everyone was terrified"
I'm listening very curiously.

"All the people in my office were running for the doors, the elevators, the steps. Everyone wanted to rush downstairs, out on the streets, outside somehow. I was also running down until I stood in front of the building. A huge 'boom' and the second plane crashed into the second tower. I have seen it, because I was just looking up to the first one. Then, suddenly, I heard a dull bounce not far from me. Someone jumped out of the window, dropped on the pure concrete and was lying dead on the street right before me. Then the second one fell, then the third. People were jumping out of the building. Everybody was screaming around me. I just starred at the scene, paralyzed."

I remember that. I followed these pictures on TV back in Berlin. But only after I got home from the Olympic Stadium that day. When the attacks happened, I have just been on a horse, riding the training of our national trainer. Then, on a certain point of time, the vice president of the federation showed up and said:
"Hey there, back in New York, someone flew with a plane into a house", and that sounded like, 'ey dude, yesterday I spilled some coffee on the table'.
"So? Matthias Rust landed a plane on the red square in Moscow", I replied before my trainer ordered me not to talk during the training session and to be concentrated.

None of us had a clue about the dimension and seriousness of this disaster at that point. I only understood it after I got home and watched the impacts of the planes and the collapsing of the towers on TV. I watched the news all night that night. I didn't do anything else. I did not sleep. I did not eat. And I also remember that I have seen people panicking, jumping out of the towers. Through Sam I'm seeing all these pictures again. Now through the eyes of someone who were standing right in front of them.

"It was a nightmare", Sam continued. "Somehow unreal, but it all happened, right before my eyes. I haven't been able to react at all. No way. I didn't run, either. I just stood there, watched how one body after another crashed on the asphalt until I could hear a huge crack from one of the towers. First I looked up. Then I looked at the man beside me. A firefighter.

"RUN!" He screamed right into my face.

I immediately turned around and ran. Then a noise from the first tower. The steal gave in and the building collapsed. It was so loud, entire Manhattan must have heard it, I'm sure."

He pauses. I don't say anything because I don't want to interrupt his thoughts and feelings.

"Do you know the sound of chalk squeaking on the chalkboard?" He asks me.

"Ja."

"Imagine this noise times thousand."

We don't say anything for a while. The highway to Atlanta seems to be endless and the landscape of this area doesn't seem to be the most exciting at that time of the year either. It looks sad actually. But maybe I only see it that way, because of the things we're just talking about. Sam:

"I randomly ran through the streets. I just ran away to somewhere. Shortly after the first, the second tower collapsed. Again: This noise. All the nicely styled, dressed in finest suits and ties banker, who all worked on their computers not even an hour ago, were running wildly, aimlessly through Manhattan. I was one of them. Nobody knew what would happen next. We were all afraid; afraid to death. Fear was written in the face of everybody. It was terrible."

Silence. I look at Sam. He notices it but doesn't look back at me. He holds his view strictly directed on the highway.

Only now I realize how beautiful he actually is. His dark hair is nicely cut, short, but not too short to see how full and shiny it is. It falls in smooth waves over his head. Once in a while a few wisps of hair slide over his forehead but they never cover his eyes.

His skin is smooth and impeccable with a nice, light brown taint we white, pale people would need to go to the tanning studio for, or bake in the sun for days. But to him it is naturally given. It's perfect.

He is about 5'7", slim but not too skinny, his clothes are neat. Leger is not his style. Not even on a ride like this one.

"I was hit. Smallest splinters of glass and smallest spalls of that building must have hit me, because I was bleeding. My arms were cut as well as parts of my lower leg and parts of my back. You can still see the scars.

I remembered that this guy I know was living somewhere around that area. I walked a few blocks and rang the doorbell. He was there, probably fled home, I don't know. He opened the door and asked me in. That's all I remember. Then I passed out."

Sam's eyes stick to the street, but I'm not sure if he really consciously looks at it or not. I just listen to him and don't say anything. So far I've never talked to anybody who has really been at the scene and was able to report from there. I just know that the 9/11 attacks hit me extraordinarily hard. I've felt like dazed, for days.

Ever since then I basically associate New York with that event. New York means to me the attacks of the world trade center. And now this: Meeting someone who has been there, a survivor. He says that his life has completely changed after that. Not immediately though, but within further month. The deeper it sank in, the more he internalized what had happened, the more things changed.

"The days after the attack have been remarkably quiet in New York. You could hear that the city was mourning in shock. We bankers were working days and nights during the following weeks. All kinds of buildings were bought and sold, investments withdrawn, existing contracts backtracked and new signed. It was crazy busy in the offices. Our business continued throughout the terror.

I worked all the time even though I was injured. After nine month I become so sick that I left my carrier, left America, headed straight east. But I did not go to Madras. I went to the Dalai Lama in Dharmsala. I stayed there for about a year. This is how long I needed to recover, at least physically.

I'm suffering from that strange kind of guilt, that I survived and others had to die. They call it 'survivors guilt'. Have you heard about it?"

"Ja, I have. We've talked about it in Psychology class."

I don't remember the exact example our Prof gave us,

but I know that it hasn't been 9/11. Wired phenomena: One would believe that people are happy when they have survived a catastrophe; but mostly that's not the case. The survivors do suffer from guilt. Badly. They feel guilty that they live and the others don't. Up to that extend where they get physically sick. Just as Sam did.

Is that *his* karma? Just as predeterminated as my life history was for me? Maybe. Possibly. It seems that we all have to suffer at a certain point of time, at least once in our lives; maybe just because it is a part of it, one facet within the endless possibilities of human experiences.

For a while, it is still in the car. No one talks. We are just driving down the highway, passing the border of the State of Georgia. On the one hand I'm fascinated by my trip to the States, on the other hand I'm deeply touched and captured by the pictures that appear in my head through Sam's story.

"You know", I'm saying, "I believe, the worst moments in life are the ones that confront us with violence, outrage against humanity and death. It seems like they're leaving the deepest trail of all. They have the potential to cause serious damage anyway, that I know. And maybe that is because we can't actually explain it. Maybe because death is so unbelievable and so far away that we can't picture it, no matter how hard we try. It might be omnipresent though, but the image of it is not there. We just don't know and that's why there is no certainty. Death always was and will always be this big mysterious cloud hanging over life, remaining unrevealed for us humans. No matter what all the philosophies say and all the holy scriptures are claiming. Nobody knows what will happen after death. And the process of dying has nothing in common with life, and violence has nothing in common with the humanly longing for affection, love and security, even though this is what everyone wishes for somehow. That's what life is all about, don't you think?"

Sam looks at me. I'm looking back for a few moments. Than he says:

"How about you? Who are *you*? Just tell me something about your life."

"Is that so important?" I ask.

Sam laughs:

"Why? You don't want to tell me who you are? Maybe you're from the secret service, or the FBI? Should I worry?"

"Maybe."

"You told me something about horses. What about that? Why are you studying medicine and plan to get out of this business?"

"I hated the way people treated the animals. It was terrible. The sport-stables I've seen are like concentration camps for horses. They torture them. They use them for their own satisfaction, for their personal success, for money. They pressure them in ways you don't want to know until they break."

"What do you mean 'break'?"

"Winston, for instance. He was to be traded as *the* talent of the year, some years back. Showjumping. So he was supposed to get sold through one of the big auctions in Germany, the one in the stadium. But on a certain point, they pulled the obstacles so high during training that he got afraid and blocked. He didn't do a single jump anymore. I don't know exactly what they've done to him, but in the end he was not even represented on the show. Instead, they just left him behind after the auction was over.

Before anyone leaves a so called 'super-talent' behind, you can be sure that they've tried all they could to make this horse 'work'. And there are much more things you can do to harm a horse than just beat it with a stick."

"I don't want to know."

"You don't, believe me!

They called Mr. Goldberg, our national trainer from the pentathlon team and asked him if he wanted to have Winston. Otherwise he would have gone to the butcher.

Goldberg agreed but didn't realize that Winston was left right there. Two days later, one of the workers who was about to undo the tents that were used as stables by the auctioneers, found him.

Winston was badly injured and completely crazy by that time. They must have tortured him in, God knows, what ways.

Mr. Goldberg had an operation on his hip the same time and could not take care of him personally. And this horse was too crazy for the athletes. This is when I came into the picture."

"Did *he* asked you?"

"Yes."

"How did he know you?"

"In horse business people know each other. He must have heard that I quit the job in northern Germany and that I'm back in Berlin, officially dropping out of the big sport. So he called me."

"And that's why you're in the stadium?"

"Exactly."

"How long are you there now?"

"Almost six years."

"And Winston? Is he still there?"

"Ja, otherwise I wouldn't be there anymore either. I'm only still doing horses because of him. And then Mr. Goldberg asked me if I'm interested to train the team, too, because he travels a lot, building pentathlon teams all over the world. He just started the Guatemala-branch. I agreed, so I was in.

But that's only part-time and sporadically. Not full time thankfully. I wouldn't have taken the job otherwise. But realizing how the big business works and how violent people can be, still hurts when I think about it."

"What about your college? You are going for holistic medicine, right?"

"Yes."

"And?"

"Truth?"

"Truth!"

"I hate it!"

"How come?"

"Studying this dry shit like anatomy, pathology, physiology, I get sick even looking at my books. I'm doing it only because I don't know what else I should do. Horses are gone. That's not an option anymore. Medicine won't be it, that I know. Psychology?" I'm shaking my head, "is interesting, that's all. Impossible for me to imagine playing psychologist all day. I have no idea what to do with my life. I have no idea what I should make out of it. I have no idea what I'm here for."

43

Sam's Sister is married to a man from Taiwan. Meta also has a degree from IIT in Chennai and leads, compared to her brother from Charlotte, a quite modern household. She is a woman who got to know independence and freedom and decided very consciously against a life in India. She has a child, too. A daughter who is just a few weeks old when we go visit her. The house she lives in is big and spacious. Her husband works and she takes care of the child. But she has had a career. She had a job with a lot of responsibility and is very well educated. The first conversation I have with her is all about her being unhappy that she had to give up on her job and that she can't work anymore right now. Her thoughts are constantly circling around the gap between the child and her career. After all: Pretty western thoughts I know from friends back home.

After two days at Meta's, which were very pleasant, we're going back to New York. It's early afternoon when the skyline of this tremendous city is visible and the plane is about to touch down.

My luggage was found. As we arrive at John F. Kennedy Airport, we're getting informed that we can pick it up. Out of a mountain of suitcases I pull mine out of it, that looks obviously damaged.

We're going straight to the taxi stand in front. Obviously he knows the way well. He travels a lot. Flying is so normal and ordinary for him like for other people taking the car or the bus. No matter if there is an appointment, a business meeting or just a friend or family member to be visited, the plane is used as his main source of transportation. Money doesn't matter. Distances don't matter. He is a cosmopolitan. The entire world is his home.

For me, on the contrary, long ways to far away countries always seemed to be unreachable. But from his perspective, long distances, all these thousands and thousands of miles, are shrinking to nothing more but a quick check-in on the airport.

We're sitting in a taxi, driving towards 83rd street and Lexington Avenue. This is where one of his brothers has an apartment. Sunil is his name. He went to his parents for Christmas. Not to celebrate there, but because there is not much going on in Manhattans business during the holidays and even consultants and investment banker give themselves a few moderate days, which are the only one of this kind they have a year. Given they do business in Manhattan. For Indian bankers who are doing business with Asia, the situation is entirely different.

India does not really celebrate Christmas. There are a few, rare events, especially for children from rich families, but basically it is a normal working season like all the other months of the year as well. This is why our taxi does not go straight from the airport to the apartment Sam is staying in, but past Lexington straight to his office, Madison avenue, 54th street.

During the ride from the airport to the office I'm basically stuck to the window; but still, I can't see the top of the skyscrapers, this is how tall they are.

Even streets that have three or four lanes on every side, almost seem to be small alleys in relation to the huge buildings. Sam is talking on the phone while I can't take my eyes from the streets. Our drive through Charlotte and Atlanta has been a drive through another world. Here I'm definitely on another planet. Again.

We reach Sam's office and take the elevator up to the 39th floor.

There are different rooms, Sam's office is one of them. He immediately vanishes behind his computer. I'm going to the next room which is almost empty. It has huge windows. A wooden desk and a matching chair is the only inventory. I don't pay much attention to it, put down my bag down and go to the window. The view is phenomenal. It is already dark outside but the streets are brightly illuminated. Around us there are countless skyscrapers, bright rooms, offices where people are working.

What an absurd feeling to be in the 39th floor of a building. I've never been that high up in the air. Cars, people, intersections down on the streets seem to be infinitesimal small, and the same time I'm looking at people the same eye-level floor like myself, being not further away than the other side of the street.

The rows of shops shine bright lighted in the colors of the entire spectrum. Huge advertisements and illuminated store windows. I can hear the noise from the streets through the thick glass that interfuses with the whirring of the air condition. The windows are not to open. Fresh air only comes into the building through the central air condition system. How they get oxygen into the streets? I have no idea.

There are a very few trees staying on the sidewalk. They are fully covered with lights, up to the last little twig, constantly blinking in green, red and yellow. The trees look more like retainers that got installed only to hold this kind of electric decorations.

They appear like toy trees from up here. I'm looking into a synthetic world where there is not much room for nature. There is the central park but I believe that it is not only set up to be some kind of attraction, but to make sure that the people here won't suffocate one day.

But, of course, New York *is* fascinating. We're leaving the office a few hours later, going downstairs, looking for a taxi. They are going around in such great numbers that we only have to wait at the sidewalk, holding up one hand. Mostly one doesn't have to wait longer than a minute until a car veers from the flow of traffic and stops.

We're going from Madison and 54th to Lexington and 83rd, to the apartment of his brother. There is not only central-airconditioning and central-heating in New York, but also central apartment management. Rental contracts are always valid for one year. That means, if one rents an apartment, he has to live there for at least that period of time. When the year is over, a new contract has to be signed. Ever since Sam is just about to go back to India, it doesn't make sense for him to rent a new place. Besides, they cost a sick amount of money every month. The little one-room-apartment his brother lives in costs 3500,- Dollars a month. An this is not even down town, but in the upper east side, a relatively quiet area compared to the business area we've been to earlier.

Even though Sam is a banker today, he still sees himself as the little Madras boy, worrying about every cent, because money has always been an issue. In his understanding, it'll probably always be that way.

44

The next day Sam has to work, too. Before he leaves the apartment in the morning, he shows me a diner directly in front of our door on the other side of the street. Then he rushes out, takes a taxi and goes heading down town.

I'm staying back alone and know, that's what I'll be - for the rest of the day. I've a lot of time and after I got ready, took a shower and got dressed, I'm going downstairs right into the scenery of this American mega-city.

My first way takes me to the little diner that Sam showed me. There are all kinds of such restaurants all over Manhattan, which are called '*Diner*' - breakfast. Because they serve all day nothing else than that.

I go cross the street and enter and seat myself. I'm looking out of the window. There are houses with fire-escapes on the outside, that are typical for this city and which I've seen several times in movies.

I don't need to worry about money. Not now anyway. Sam gave me one of his credit cards so I won't be without any support as long as he's gone. Of course I can support myself and definitely have the money to afford breakfast, but in Sam's mind I don't.

I did not quite understand the financial dimension of his life at that point of time, but I am already released from my constant worries about money. I don't have to worry about how much I spend and what kind of expenses and bills are waiting at home, that want to be paid. All these thoughts, all these worries and anxieties, are falling off of me completely.

I feel free and understand very quickly that this would be the gift from him to me: Freedom; the freedom from the constant fear about how to pay for basic necessities of life. Suddenly I feel relieved from the deep worries I have known my entire life, of how to manage my existence, of how to pay for my expenses, of how to support myself. This fear followed me for I don't know how long already and it caused so many sleepless nights that I stopped counting them. But now I'm free. Totally relieved from it all.

Despite of all the noise of this huge city, peace settles within my soul.

45

All seems to be like a dream. I'm getting a little taste of the fulfillment of my dreams of freedom and detachment from worldly constraints. I don't *have* to do anything anymore. Everything is there and it's taken care of. I can do whatever I want without the pressure that I have to get anything done, without the need to do certain things, to follow a schedule. I can feel ground under my feet. My own little life in Teltow moves further and further away. It's only four weeks ago that I took off to India, searching for my Leaf, and now I'm walking through the streets of Manhattan, past gigantic buildings, Hot-dog stands and endless taxi-cascades that are filling the streets and the life I have lived feels decades ago. Even though it's only four weeks ago that I've lived an entirely different life. It's only four weeks ago that I've been such a slave to my limited feelings, my limited thoughts, my limited life.

I'm strolling along the sidewalks and can hardly believe to be here. It is winter and cold but I don't really feel the coldness, this is how fascinated I am. I'm passing by a countless number of shops that are based in the ground floors of the houses and which look like they have been there since the beginning of last century, or maybe even longer.

What I never realized until now is the fact, that here, in this city, the Second World War practically did not take place. There has never been such mass destruction as it has in Berlin. The very ordinary houses, simple apartment buildings and businesses have not been bombed. So I can see that the average house and the average shop is much older than the ones I usually walk by in Germany.

I'm entering a little Bakery through a wooden door that looks like it was build just when the shop was founded, estimated somewhere between 1900 and 1920. The door is warped and creaks as I open it. The door-knob is worn out throughout the years; the color, that was obviously renewed a few times, peels off on a few spots. The sign that is installed on the outside and says 'Bakery' looks also as if it is the original one from around 1920. The appearance of the shop tells about many decades of history.

Manhattan has an historical charm that I never expected to find here. Of course there are no churches from 1200 or castles from the 6th or 7th century, but the average building looks like it is 100 years old or even older. This we don't have in our cities that were all somehow rebuilt after the war with the least effort possible. We're looking into cold and lifeless facades from the 50th, 60th and 70th which are, because of the lack of money and taste, 'decorated' with bald walls and a bare concrete cover. Or in even newer complexes of buildings, housing areas or industrial estates, which got built in former East-Germany somewhere on the ground of deforested woods and fields and that are just as ugly as all the other ones. But the historical charm that we like to deprive the Americans of is basically exactly what we ourselves don't have; that we don't have anymore anyway. Our history may exist and visible on a few selected places, but it got basically destroyed completely and erased from our everyday life. One only has to look at the pictures of Berlin after the last war. They are telling all.

Not that there are no modern houses in Manhattan; of course there are. But they were added to an existing city that grew ever since the first man settled here. They have not been built out of necessity because everything else was bombed to the ground. And they are not like most of the ones in Germany, build as fast and cheap as possible, but with investors, putting millions of dollars and many thoughts into well designed architecture. This is why even the modern buildings have a totally different character than the pale skylines in Germany.

My legs carry me further down and I practically bathe in the impressions that force themselves on me. But I'm not part of all this. Again I feel like being only a quiet observer. I'm free and unbound. I don't work. I have to go nowhere, do nothing, get nothing done. I'm just here, feeling the whole intensity of the moment, feeling true and real freedom. I believe to feel it anyway.

I pass Lexington Avenue, heading west, going to Park Avenue, then to Madison and finally reach 5th, that goes directly along the east side of Central park. I am walking all the way down to 59th. This is where the upper east side ends. Now I'm in Midtown, walking further down south and reaching Madison Square Park where 5th Avenue and Broadway meet. The Broadway goes all across Manhattan.

It is almost an entire day-walk that takes me from 83rd to 23rd , but I don't feel exhausted. It is my excitement that drives me further and further through the streets of New York I can't see enough of.

I'm following the Broadway, traversing Soho, Chinatown and reach Trinity. Just before I get to the financial district I'm taking a break. I'm looking for a Diner at City Hall Park. It doesn't take me long to find one. I'm taking a long, nice break and order a big glass freshly squeezed orange juice and a few scrambled eggs with toast.

While I eat I can feel this deep, comfortable inner peace that already came over me this morning and which I prayed for before I went to India. I'm feeling peaceful and content. Even though I'm 'only' watching the everyday life on the streets and nothing out of the ordinary happens, it is still very extraordinary to me. I watch taxis driving, salesman selling and people walking, talking, laughing. Nothing special for the ones living here. And I have to admit that I've seen those kind of scenes uncountable times back in my own home country. But here it all takes place in another world and is therefore new and different.

Island of Manhattan

After about an hour of eating, drinking and looking-out-of-the-window I pay and leave the restaurant. I'm taking off another direction, away from the park, away from the Broadway, go down Chamber Street, cross Church Street and again reach the Broadway, but this time the West-Broadway. I'm looking down south and can see: At the end of it, there are no more houses. I must be reaching the south tip of the Island.

After a few blocks the street ends. Immediately my knees get shaky because I'm just realizing where my trip took me. I'm going along Vesey Street back to Church again, going round that areal and now stay between Trinity Plaza and Liberty Street, directly in front of Ground Zero and stare into the emptiness right in front of me.

This is where the twin towers were standing. This is the corner where the pictures came from, that went all around the world on September 11.

I have no idea how long I'm staying there, but I'm staying there for quite a while. My adventure is over and I'm moving very slow, up and down the street, my view tacked to the emptiness before me, my head full of pictures and thoughts.

The world trade center doesn't exist anymore. I've seen the scenes I don't know how often in the news, in papers, in videos, on the internet. Of course I know that. But now I can see it with my own eyes. I'm staying right where once the two of the tallest towers of the world went right up into the sky and look into a foundation pit.

46

Sam calls. I take the phone he gave me out of my bag and answer:

"Where are you?" He instantly asks.

"In Trinity", I say, "I took a walk."

"All the way down there?" His voice sounds amazed. "That's far. You must be very tired. Do you wanna have dinner? Are you hungry?"

I'm starving actually. Now that he asks I can feel *how* hungry and tired I am. It is already dark and spotlights illuminate the excavators and cranes.

"Take a taxi", he says without waiting for my answer, "and come to Lexington and 28th. There is a South Indian restaurant. I'll introduce you to uncle Khania. In about an hour?"

"Okay", I quickly say.

"Okay, bye than." I only hear a slight click through the phone and the line is already disconnected.

The short call ripped me out of my thoughts. I immediately turn around and turn to the street behind me.

To find a taxi is no problem. I get in and reach the restaurant almost exactly an hour after we spoke. Sam is already there. He's talking loudly with one of the waiters. His name is Mahindra and I pick up that he belongs to the family of the uncle.

"Hey, you must be Antonia. Sammy has already talked me into the ground. He's taking about you none-stop", Mahindra jokes and reaches out his hand to welcome me. I reply but only manage a short:

"Yes", and grin.

"What did you say?", he says as he turns right back to

Sam, "You met her on a plane?"

"Who sold you the ticket?", one of the guys behind the bar shouts.

"Which flight?", the second barkeeper asks.

"Which airline?", Mahindra is clinging in.

Sam is laughing and filled with pride, pulls me close to him, turns to me and says:

"I'm happy that you're here."

Just as we are going to sit down, uncle Khania is coming towards us.

"Sammy", he says with arms outspread, "couldn't you have warned us that you bring such a beautiful woman! We would have at least got some descend clothes, yehar!"

Again the entire crew is laughing. This show is ready to go on stage. All of them, without exception, look absolutely terrific. Mahindra, a well dressed, tall man with an Indian taint, wears pleat-front trousers, a noble shirt and above it a west matching his pants. He almost looks like he came right from the 1920th. The barkeepers are making a similar impression. But the uncle is the crown of the crew: He is, already in his 60's, a suit model for Hugo Boss in New York. Once in a while there are huge placates hanging all around the city on which he is to see in all his sublimity and elegance. There is something majestic about uncle Khania. We hardly sit when Sam whispers in my ear:

"Uncle makes a million dollars a year in profit."

I'm still smiling. Sam automatically does business talk with me. This is probably how he talks with his colleagues because these are things an investment banker should know. And Sam knows them. He knows the yearly revenue of all kinds of companies, who sponsors who, what money goes where and who is financially related to whom in terms of economics, politics, worldwide. He explains to me the context between certain politicians and the laws their pass, which married couples are sitting in what lobbies and why certain resolutions are rejected, others adopted.

I'm always spell bound by Sam's stories when he lifts the curtain and lets a few secrets show about confidential information and internal affairs. When Sam is not totally tired and wasted, he is a brilliant talker. He amuses me, night after night.

Dinner is short and time goes by quick. We're tired; Sam from work, I from the long tour and the impessions I still need to digest. But I keep them to myself and don't mention Ground Zero. I don't want to wake Sam's memories and feelings. And mine neither. Not now.

47

Sam is getting up early again, leaving the house, taking a taxi, going to the office. This time I'm going with him. Sam is talking on the phone. I'm thinking myself back to the Palm Leafs.

I did not do everything I was told to by the Leafs. The last task is still undone: I did not go to a St. Mary's Church on a Saturday, I did not pray. This task will probably remain unfulfilled. Today is the last day of the year. It's only hours until the year is over. Will it destroy the mystery of the Leafs that I did not take the last step? Will it do damage to my soul? And will the prophecies of the Palm Leaf Reader not come true then?

It is the end of a year, were one experience was greater and more fascinating than the other. I somehow do feel an urge to go somewhere and speak some prayers. I want to thank the creator, the universe, destiny or whatever, for all the fantastic experiences I was allowed to make and which I came out of renewed and healed. The experiences given to me were so extraordinary that I feel thankful when I think about how dramatically my life changed within a few weeks, how unexpectedly new paths opened. My trip to the US is, of course, a part of it all.

"I know where you can go. It's a place close to my office", Sam quickly says between two phone calls, shortly before we reach his office.

The taxi takes us a few blocks further down to Madison and 51st. There he drops me and leaves.

I find myself right in front of the famous St. Patrick Cathedral. I'm walking slowly up the steps to the main portal.

On the other side of the street I can see a huge sculpture in front of some building. Immediately I'm recognizing this figure: It is Atlas, kneeing, carrying the world on his shoulders, symbol for the heavy burden of life. The world and its burden can be truly overwhelming. Will we ever be free from them as long as we live in this world?

A gigantic dome opens up right in front of me as I enter the cathedral. Stunning. Monumental. Simply fantastic. I'm walking slowly along the rows of benches, under the stony vault, to the altar room. There are long corridors on each side that also do go straight to the altar room but the same time to an areal behind it, big enough to hold a few hundred people.

St. Patrick's Cathedral, New York 2006

But this one is not directed to a Jesus cross as the main part of the cathedral, but to some kind of statue. The closer I come the better I see that it is the statue of the holy mother Mary. So, St. Patrick's is a Jesus *and* a St. Mary's church.

My knees are giving in and I sink on one of the benches, fixating the sculpture of the holy mother.

Unbelievable! Tears are running over my face which I hardly sense. They are happening to me just as every single bit that had anything to do with the library happened to me. Without me doing a thing. December 31 of the year 2005 is a Saturday. I'm only realizing now.

An old woman must have watched me because she comes cross the church, sits down beside me and says: "When a life period reaches its end it also means, that something new begins. Life is not over because different times and phases come and go. They are like the seasons which constantly change and which follow one another, which cause each other, maybe even emerge with each other. But in the end they're making a lifetime colorful and multifarious. This is why things and incidents, that touch our heart, are like shining stars on the firmament of our memory. They light up the darker parts of our way and sometimes brighten the racking uncertainty of our existence. They give us strength and faith."

I'm looking straight in her eyes. She returns my view for a few moments and smiles, taking her hand and stroking me carefully along the head, along the cheek, but she doesn't touch me. Her hand slides a few centimeters away from me down. Then she gets up, her eyes still directed towards mine, nods as a sign of valediction, turns around and leaves the chapel through one of the side exits. I'm watching her leaving and still look at the door for a while after it's already closed. Her presence is still sensable.

So this is what the Palm Leafs were talking about. Have they known about this woman? Were we already supposed to meet, long before it even happened?

I raise my view. It is quiet inside of me. Not even my inner voice is audible. Nothing. There is only me, the image of the holy mother and this thoughtless emptiness that fills the room.

Now this is where the journey of the Palm Leaf Library finds its end. Now I've done all the things I was meant to do and which were delivered through the chapter Diksha. All that was meant to be done and experienced fulfilled itself, seemingly without my assistance. The deed is done.

48

New year in New York. Sam wants me to stay. I insist to take my flight back to Germany on January 8. The last days of my stay I basically spend alone. Questions arise which are waiting for answers since many years. What do I want to make out of my life?

The one and only thing that remained steady throughout all times and all changes is me and my music. It is not the end of all my longings but it feels so familiar doing it that it is able to give me some comfort.

I've got enough experiences of all kinds of musical engagements that I feel able to organize a little event.

Back when Sam was still just a voice on the phone the idea of a benefit concert in Teltow was born. I want to tell about the libraries, show pictures, play piano. This is supposed to be my small contribution that I would like to give to *that* country, that changed my life within only two weeks entirely.

Shortly after I arrived in Teltow I can't stop thinking about Alexander. Am I ready to open up to a new man like I opened up to my husband? Will I ever be able to love someone the way I loved him? Is it right to have someone else by my side? But what if I don't open up anymore and stay hidden behind bars just the way I do ever since Alexander died? Do I want to be alone forever? I longed for a companion, a friend. For Sam. I wished for him and the wish came true. And he fascinates me, too. His life fascinates me. His stories; and the way he looks at the world, which seems to have no borders for him. It also feels good to see how happy my presence makes him. But I don't really know what I should do anyway. Is Sam really this kind of man and will I really find this kind of India in Bombay that I was so deeply touched by? I will probably only know it when I dared to get to know him better, him and his life, him and Bombay.

This is why I'm leaving Germany, going back to the States two weeks later.

This time I'm staying longer. Sam is working from early in the morning to late afternoon and I'm, basically, alone all the time. In this megacity I don't know anyone. I'm just as alone as I already feel. Only my fascination for this new, different world, as well as the impressions and things that happened over the last weeks, are still with me, protecting me.

Sam and I are hardly seeing each other. The evenings we spend together are short. Most of the time we are in some restaurant, having dinner. He is tired from his long, stressful days, wants to eat and sleep to be refreshed for the next day. But the little time we have is fantastic. We're laughing a lot, telling stories, understanding each other. It's nice to be with him even though the few hours we have pass by much too fast.

49

Sam wants to marry me. I don't answer. That's way too overhasty I think. I can't make a decision that big so quickly.

He's already gone when I awake the next morning. Today I'm not going for a walk, but take the subway to Battery Park and take a ferry and leave Manhattan. The tour is going to the statue of liberty and Ellis Island.
The trip is been offered as a package. Both islands are lying beside each other. So it is the ideal thing to make the tourists see both at once. I've seen the statue of liberty on pictures many times, the name 'Ellis Island' I'm hearing for the first time.
The little ferry takes about half an hour. It goes back and forth between the islands all day long. It's raining and the sea is rough. I'm sitting in one, big room under deck. A dove got caught in here by mistake, fearfully running around the floor, flattering once in a

while wildly around. It tries to find a way out, to the freedom it belongs to.

I'm afraid of the thought about living in this new world that would be ahead of me if I gave in and say yes to Sam. Because my future would not be in America, which I got a taste of during the last weeks, but in Bombay. Of course I don't know Bombay, but I know Madras and it scares me to imagine that I'd have to live in this strangeness. But what is the alternative? A life in Teltow, that appears to me so limited and closed-minded that I almost feel sick when I only think about it? My little hometown makes me feel that I have to suffocate when I imagine to spend the rest of my life there? That can't be my future! I simply won't allow that to be my future! Absolutely impossible. It already seems that I don't know anyone anymore out of all the people who have been a part of my life for so long. There is this experience between us that separates us now; that will always separate us and that can't be taken back.

No matter how I look at it, the life I had is over and world I lived in doesn't exist anymore. Nor for me.

50

What is the matter with me that I seriously think about spending a lifetime with a man I only know a few weeks? Is the longing for another world really that big that I consider to give my life into the hands of an almost stranger? Is the burden of my own existence really so heavy that I prefer the totally unknown, instead of the familiar? Hoping that it'll hold a new life for which I know I would never have in Teltow?

Fact is that I don't have a fundament to my life. Once, long ago, it used to be the horse business, emotionally as well as financially, but that is past. I feel hollow, my life empty and up to this day I never found anything that was able to fill this empty space in my life and inside of myself.

And all of a sudden there is Sam, who reaches out to me and wants to marry me, unknown; the Indian way though. It is common for Indians to make a decision wether they want to spend their life with someone or not, very quickly. The philosophy behind it is, that there is no perfect relationship anyway but only the ability to accept doubtless whatever is given to us, the ability to give ourselves into something entirely and wishlessness. These are the things that are important if one wants to be happy after all. Not the other person, but only we, ourselves, have the power to solve our karma and to live up to our real purpose. *This only* can bring true satisfaction and inner peace. As long as we search outside of us, as long as we want someone else to make us happy, we will automatically head into chaos and unhappiness. The solution to inner imbalances always lays within ourselves. Only the development of awareness and the focus of the spirit to a higher truth than we can understand, contains salvation and fortitude. And it depends on us, if we take the chance to rise to a higher level of understanding, or if we don't.

That is, anyway, what the holy scriptures of India are saying and Sam knows them well. And ever since he likes me and we understand each other well, it is clear to him that he wants to marry me. In addition to that, it is written that destiny is not in our hands anyway and that life is only manageable with trust and faith in wise, godly guidance.

I'm pretty familiar with this philosophy; I've studied it for many years. That's why Sam doesn't only understand me and the pictures I carry inside but I, in return, understand him and the understanding he is living in.

Such an understanding of life is alien for most people in New York. The Americans have their own philosophy just so have the Germans. But Sam is not an American even though he is just about to receive the American citizenship. That's why he's alone, too, in his own way.

We searched and found each other. And, maybe, I'm thinking about a life with him because our connection is so destined, so right. It is out of question. It just happened to us. It is just there. It just exists. Maybe it has always existed long before we even met?

Only one thing is certain: Whatever will happen, whatever I'll decide, I will be alone – in Germany in one way, with Sam in India another way. And that's why it somehow doesn't matter which way I'll choose: Loneliness and isolation are waiting. They are inescapable ahead of me, no matter if I want them or not.

51

The ferry lands and I'm leaving the boat. Ellis Island. I'm looking at a red clinker building with white ornaments on the side. I can see the Statue of Liberty from here, that has been our first stop and which we have just visited and I just touched some minutes ago. Behind it: The panorama of Manhattan.

The main building is aligned with the harbor. Stony stairways are going right up to the entrance. I'm walking towards it and go inside. A mountain of old suitcases, bags and baskets welcome me as I come in. I look around. Nobody is here. I keep on walking, entering a hall just as huge as the first one.

Ellis Island is a museum. An 'immigration museum'. On huge boards, that are put up on the walls and on certain displayed items is described, what this place is all about, what history stays behind it, how it came to be.

Throughout decades, the island served as a central collecting point for people who came from all countries of the world to immigrate to the United States. The suitcases and bags are remaining luggage from the last century, from people who never reached the new land, their final destination.

The halls are huge and cold. It is an office. It was the central immigration office of the United States. It used to serve as such for many years.

The house is a two-story building. Upstairs it has big rooms, downstairs there are gigantic halls. They are build to dispatch 500.000 people every year. But at certain times the number of arrivals counted up to 12.000 people a day.

View from Ellis Island to the Statue of Liberty

View from the harbor into New York's Skyline

Sometimes it took several weeks until the travelers have been through all required and necessary procedures such as medical examinations, psychological testings, questionings and perusals of all demanded documents, before they could leave the Island. Everyone who came here could get randomly sorted out. Medical reports were authored based on which everybody got a sign painted on his shoulder. The signs classified: An *S* for senility, *CT* for an eye disease, an *X* for all kinds of psychic disorders. Sick, poor and political extremists, previously convicted and illiterates were not allowed to enter the country.

Many people died within these cold walls, because they couldn't resist the flood of bacteria caused by the lack of hygiene during their long trips they took from their home countries to this place. This is why Ellis Island is also called the 'Isle of Tears'.

10% already died on the ships themselves, which sometimes were lying in the harbor for days. This was when the crew did not get permission to go on land, because Ellis Island was hopelessly overcrowded. The New Yorkers called these ships 'swimming coffins' or 'coffin-ships'.

On this Island, destiny was decided. Hopes were born and dreams buried, families got ripped apart and brothers and sisters got split up. The circumstances under which immigrants came here must have been disastrous, but the people took all the risks.

What kind of desperation drove them to this place?

What kind of desperation drives *me* to this place? The search for the answer to the question, if I should leave the old world behind and dare to take the step into an unknown new one. The idea, the hope, the possibility,

197

that there might be an entire different life for me and that it might be worth to let go of what I have. This is what drove me here, to Ellis Island. This is what drove all the other people here, who, long ago, past through these halls, where their destiny was decided. So is now mine.

I go to the upper floor through a gallery of pictures that show people who have been here and who have been just at that point in their life, that I am at right now. I'm looking in their faces, in their eyes, recognizing myself. I am not alone. I'm not alone with the decision that made me come here. I'm just one of thousands of people who have been here before, to make exactly the one step in life that I'm now thinking to make.

98% of the immigrants were allowed to enter the 'promised land'. After passing the procedures, they became citizens of the United States Of America. Their new lives began as they left the boat that took them over to Manhattan. They made their decision. They came here, ready to even pay with their lives for the chance to begin a new one, in a new world. Sometimes with not more than 20 dollars in their pockets.

It can't be just a coincidence that I ended up on Ellis Island. It can't be just an accident that let me here. '… some important thoughts will be coming to you and that will help you make an important decision', have been the last words of the Palm Leaf Reader in Madras, only a few weeks ago on the other side of the world.

Ellis Island is, of course, not a natural, but an artificial island to serve as a 'gateway into a new world' for those who dared to go through it. The life of every second American can be backtracked to this place.

And now I'm staying here, in front of the coastline of Manhattan, at the probably most distinctive place there is in this world to leave everything behind and step right into a new life. Because this island is unique. Such place doesn't exist in this world a second time, anywhere else.

I slowly understand that the ferry that will leave the isle of tears today will take another person into a new life. Because the decision is clear. The decision is clear and obvious. The decision to dare a completely new life was made before I could make it. The message of the island has reached me and I give in to the destiny that seems to be predetermined.

There is a little cafe in the first floor. Before I leave the island I'm going there to let all these impressions sink in. How long I sit there? I don't know. It's already getting dark when I leave. As I pay for my coffee I'm asking a waiter to take a picture of me just as pictures were taken from all the people who past through these walls before. I don't have to be registered though, but I want to capture this moment. I want to hold on to it for all times, forever. It shall become immortal and one of these shining stars on the firmament of our memory, that sometimes light up the darker parts of our way and which the old lady in St. Patrick's talked about. This moment shall give me strength and faith for all that is going to come. That's what I wish for. I hope so anyway. I want it to be that way because I long for strength and faith for the future and its way to the forever unknown.

Ellis Island 2006

At the exit there is a small display of jewelry. There are no souvenirs. Even though this is a museum and so a public place, the island is not marketed to tourists. I quickly decide to take a ring with me. A small, simple ring with an orange stone, shaped as a heart, and two hands holding it. There are no other rings and nothing else either that I like. The ring fits like cast-on.

I pay, put the ring on my finger, go through the huge entrance hall, past the mountain of suitcases and baskets and step outside. The ferry that goes back to Manhattan now will take another person from an old to a new life.

It is still raining and the sea is still rough. I'm staying on deck, looking over the water. My view slides between Ellis Island and the skyline of New York back and forth. I feel the rain on my skin. Drops run down my face. It is cold.

Hudson River just mutates to the symbol of the short path between an end and a new beginning.

While I look over the water, I just understand what I learned in India: My previous life was shallow and empty, was hectic. India taught me to be faithful. It taught me to see the great treasures in the world, when they are right in front of me. It taught me to trust life. It taught me to follow my heart. And it taught me what is really important: To be thankful for what we have; to appreciate who we are meant to be and to value what is given to us. Not the possession of material goods can give our lives purpose and us satisfaction, not the fancy envelope I keep my money in, not the little ring I just bought, but the feeling to be one with the universe and to be safe in a secure, warm world full of hopes and dreams.

Antonia Katharina Tessnow, Germany 2010

About the Author:

Antonia Katharina Tessnow was born in November 15, 1975 in Berlin. After finishing the evangelic school of Steglitz in Germany she graduated from High School in Moravia, Iowa. After her one year of student exchange she returned to Germany and worked many years professionally as a horse-back-trainer. At the age of 22 she moved to the north of Germany, worked in a sports stable and specialized in dressage. There she trained and qualified horses in all level of performances.

In the age of 28 she returned to her hometown and worked in the Olympic Stadion where she worked 6 years for the national association of modern pentathlon and trained athletes in the discipline of show jumping. Extra occupational she studied holistic medicine, holistic veterinary science and holistic psychology. Furthermore she passed a three year advanced educational class on the Institute of Emotional Processing.

In her mid-30th, after finishing all her educations, she left equestrianism to take advanced educational courses at the Devi Clinic in Sri Lanka and acquired her international authorization to work holistically in medicine. In the following three years she commuted between the United States and India to lead psycho-energetic healing sessions.

Antonia Katharina is Doctor of holistic Medicine and Psychology, gained a wide spread comprehension of alternative healing methods, including the therapeutical use of music. She visited classes of one of the leading reincarnation therapists today, Trutz Hardo. During her stay in India she specialized in psycho-energetic and musical healing work, reincarnation therapy and phytomedicine.

Since 2009 she returned to Germany and dedicates her life not only to her artistical, holistic medical and authorical work but also her new found love and passion: The luxury Russian dog breed called Bolonka Zwetna.

Besides her holistic work of all kinds, which she further intensified, she trained as a groomer and completed additional education in keeping, breeding and animal lore. Today she lives close to a small village in Mecklenburg-Vorpommern, authors books and leads the professional dog breeding station called the 'Zarenhunde aus dem Alten Jagdhaus'.

Website of the Author:

www.antonia-katharina.de

Website of the Kennel
'aus dem Alten Jagdhaus':

rund-um-hunde.jimdo.com

Website of the Breeding Station `Altes Jagdhaus`:

altes-jagdhaus.jimdo.com

Silent Night, Holy Night

Memories of a Christmas Eve during the last year of World War II

a Short Story

About the Book

1943. It is Christmas. All around the world, children write diaries to somehow cope with the unbelievable experiences they are send through during wartimes and turmoil. The slightly older sister of Antonia Katharina`s mother is 9 years old when she describes the events of one single night through her childish eyes. A destiny that leaves deep impressions on ones soul and won`t leave anyone untouched.
A wonderful reminder of the peaceful times we are allowed to live in today.

About the Author

Antonia Katharina Tessnow is the daughter of a former East Prussian Family who came to Germany after World War I. Her grandparents settled in Berlin but had to flee the city together with their children after their apartment building was bombed and completely destroyed during the last year of World War II. They returned many years later to Berlin, but even though Antonia Katharina was born there, she never felt at home in this city. Today she lives in the countryside of Mecklenburg-Vorpommern.

Astro Calendar

With Ephemerides,
Planetary Charts and Moon Phases

Every year new!

The Astro-Calendar is supposed to serve as a way-wiser throughout the year. It doesn`t only provide the information needed by an astrologer, but also appeals to everyone who feels a deep connection to nature, to the tides and to the orbiting planets around us. This is why this calendar serves Hobby-Astrologers as well as professionals, whose work depends on the exact sidereal time given by the ephemerides.

In the beginning there is a blank horoscope for you to write your personal chart or any chart you wish. Further the progressions of the planets are graphically represented, also in charts, and this way visually accessible. Before each month the ephemerides for that particular time are listed, so that you always have the entire planetary positions during the entire course of the year right with you. The transitions of the sun and the moon from one sign to the next are also listed right on the corresponding days. May this calendar help all those who want to have the planetary influences, which we are all subjected to, always in sight.

Your feelings of connectedness with the universe will deepen over time and you will develop the most accurate sensitivity and gain a great understanding for the different planetary positions and their energetic influences on us and the entire world.

Die Botschaft der Tiere

Der Weg zurück zu uns selbst

Ein Wegweiser durch unsere Zeit

Es ist ganz und gar möglich, den Weg nach Hause zu finden. Wir brauchen nicht zu warten, bis wir diese Welt verlassen und zurück in unsere Seelenheimat gehen, um in den ewigen Gefilden Frieden und Liebe zu erleben. Wir können uns unser Zuhause, das Paradies, auch hier auf der Erde, auf diesem Planeten erschaffen. Es ist tatsächlich möglich, uns in ein neues, anderes Bewusstsein hineinzuentwickeln, von dem nicht nur die heiligen Schriften und die Erleuchteten im Laufe unserer Erdgeschichte berichtet haben, sondern von dem uns auch die Tiere erzählen, indem sie es uns Tag für Tag vorleben.

Wir Menschen können noch umkehren. Wir müssen diese Welt nicht zerstören. Es muss nicht alles so weitergehen wie bisher. Es ist möglich, den Weg zurück ins Paradies zu finden, doch können ihn uns nur diejenigen weisen, die ihn kennen.

Wenn wir den Tieren erlauben, uns den Weg zu weisen, werden wir ihn finden. Wenn wir ihre Botschaft ernstnehmen, sie verinnerlichen und versuchen, sie zu entschlüsseln, werden wir sie verstehen. Die Tiere haben das Paradies nie verlassen. Wer, wenn nicht sie, könnten uns diesen Weg weisen?

Kommunikation mit Tieren

ein Essay

Tierkommunikation ist keine Kunst, die nur wenigen Auserwählten vorbehalten ist, sondern eine Fähigkeit, die in jedem von uns schlummert und uns allen innewohnt. Es ist nichts, was man lernen muss, sondern es ist etwas, woran man sich erinnern kann, wenn man dafür bereit ist. Dieses kleine Büchlein beschreibt in kurzen, aufeinander aufbauenden Abschnitten die Kommunikation mit Tieren. Es soll dabei helfen, sich an seine ursprünglichen Fähigkeiten zu erinnern und sie wieder nutzbar zu machen; es soll ein Wegweiser sein und zeigen, dass jede Begegnung eine Aufgabe für uns bereit hält, für die es immer eine Lösung gibt und an der wir wachsen können. Alles hat einen Sinn und es lohnt sich, darauf zu vertrauen. Selbst wenn wir ihn manchmal nicht gleich verstehen.

Textauszug: 'Jede Kommunikation ist individuell. Jede Verbindung, jedes Karma einmalig. Manchmal sind die Tiere überhaupt erst dafür da, um dem Menschen die gefühlte, intuitive Wahrnehmung und Kommunikation zu erschließen. Es ist ein Gewinn für alle, wenn der Mensch beginnt, eine Verbindung zu seinem Tier und damit zu sich selbst herzustellen, sich seinen Themen und deren Botschaften zu öffnen und von ihnen zu lernen. Wenn du dazu bereit bist, das Tier in seiner Ganzheit zu erkennen und als gleich-wertig zu schätzen, wenn du dich auf dein Ganz-Sein einlässt und dem Tier genauso erlaubst, es selbst zu sein, wie es das Tier dir erlaubt, dann entsteht wahre Verbundenheit. Wenn du über die weit verbreiteten Trainingsmethoden der Dominanz und der autoritären Kontrolle hinauswächst und dich dem tieferen Sinn einer Begegnung zuwendest, wenn du versuchst zu erkennen, was dein Gegenüber dir beibringen will, dann beginnt die Kommunikation mit deinem Tier.

Bolonka Zwetna

*Von der Empfindsamkeit der Hundeseele
und der Liebe, die sie schenkt*

**Der Nr. 1 Bestseller in amazon in der Kategorie
'Hunde'**

Dieser kleine Ratgeber soll nicht nur zum allgemeinen Verständnis der Beziehungen von Hunden zu uns Menschen beitragen, sondern vor allem den Menschen in seiner Seele berühren. Neben kurzen Überblicken über Rassestandard, Ernährung, Fellpflege und Haltung führt die Autorin den Leser in die facettenreiche Welt der Hundeseele, die voll tiefer Empfindsamkeit ist und niemanden unberührt lässt, der die Fähigkeit besitzt, zu fühlen.

Antonia Katharinas Liebe gilt seit jeher den Tieren. Viele Jahre war sie hauptberuflich in der Reiterei tätig bevor sie Heilpraktik, ganzheitliche Psychologie und Tierheilpraktik studierte. Seitdem widmet sie ihr Leben den Kleinhunderassen im Allgemeinen und dem Bolonka Zwetna im Speziellen. Neben ihrer schriftstellerischen, musischen und tierheilpraktischen Arbeit hat sie sich auf die Auftragsmalerei von Tierfotos spezialisiert und betreut ihre kleine Rassehundezucht der 'Zarenhunde aus dem Alten Jagdhaus'.

Die Hundezucht 'aus dem Alten Jagdhaus'
präsentiert sich unter

rund-um-hunde.jimdo.com

HAIR

Alles über alternative Haarpflege

HAIR - Alles über alternative Haarpflege, ist ein heilpraktisches Sachbuch. Es gibt in den einleitenden Kapiteln einen Überblick über die Inhaltsstoffe in herkömmlichen Shampoos und Duschgels und wie schädlich synthetisch hergestellte Chemikalien in der täglichen Anwendung auf Haut und Haaren sind. Des weiteren wird auf die Langzeitschäden eingegangen, die sich durch den dauerhaften und wiederholten Kontakt mit diesen Chemikalien ergeben können.

Der Hauptteil des Buches zeigt Alternativen zu herkömmlichen Produkten auf, die leicht umzusetzen und anzuwenden sind. Es wird auf komplizierte Anwendungstechniken verzichtet und ganz gezielt die Einfachheit der Methoden betont und in den jeweiligen Anwendungsbeschreibungen dargelegt. Alle alternativen Methoden zur Haut- und Haarreinigung sind von mir persönlich im Selbstversuch getestet, für jeden Interessierten leicht nachvollziehbar und die entsprechenden reinigenden Substanzen leicht erhältlich.
Im letzten Teil des Buches wird auf die Lebensweise, die Ernährung, Öle, Haarbürsten und Tipps und Tricks eingegangen, die langfristig und nachhaltig für gesunde und volle Haare sowie für gesunde, vitale und frische Haut sorgen.

Ziel dieses Buches ist es, das Bewusstsein für den Umgang mit unserem Körper, unserer Umwelt und damit unserer Gesundheit zu schärfen.

Tattoo – Laser – Cover Up

Wenn der Traum zum Albtraum wird

Sowohl das Tätowieren als auch das Lasern ist nicht nur ein Eingriff in deinen Körper, sondern auch in deine Persönlichkeit und dem daran gekoppelten Gefühl, dir selbst gegenüber. Tätowieren verändert einen Menschen; mitunter hat diese Veränderung weitreichende Folgen und hinterlässt tiefe Spuren in deiner Seele. Festzustellen, dass dir das langersehnte Tattoo nicht gefällt oder gar misslungen ist, ist zudem eine schmerzliche Erfahrung, für die es wenig Helfende und Mitfühlende gibt.

Dieses Büchlein soll nicht nur eine Hilfestellung für Betroffene sein, sondern auch die Gedanken derer anregen, die mit der Idee spielen, sich unter die Nadel zu legen. Nicht nur meine eigenen Erfahrungen rund um das Thema Tattoo – Laser – Cover Up sind hier offengelegt, sondern es wurde auch ein Blick in all die Seelenschmerzen und inneren Qualen gewährt, die mit solchen Erfahrungen verbunden sind.

Jede Krise enthält eine Chance, weswegen die Chinesen dafür ein und dasselbe Wort verwenden. Die Chancen dieser Krise sind die daraus entsprungenen, weiterführenden und sehr hilfreichen Gedanken sowie all die wichtigen Überlegungen zum Tätowieren allgemein, die dir hoffentlich helfen mögen und die du unbedingt anstellen solltest, *bevor* du eine Entscheidung triffst, die dich in jedem Fall für dein Leben zeichnen wird.

Madras

Zauber der Palmblätter

Die Palmblattbibliotheken: Tausende Jahre alt und bis heute ein ungelöstes Rätsel. Das Geheimnis dieses Ortes ist das Thema dieses Buches. Die Geschichte dreht sich um eines der größten Rätsel der Menschheit.
Eine Reise führte mich dort hin. Ich habe meine kleine Heimatstadt verlassen um der Sagenumwobenen Legende auf den Grund zu gehen, die besagt, dass dort alle Lebensgeschichten aller Menschen niedergeschrieben sind; allerdings nur von denjenigen, die sich aufmachen, um danach zu suchen.
Eben das habe ich getan. Und dies ist es, was ich gefunden habe.

Dieses Buch liegt in deutscher und englischer Fassung vor.

Menschen, die dieses Buch gelesen haben:

"Ein interessantes Buch. Wer will, findet die Antwort auf die Frage: Wie viele Leben hat ein Mensch?"
Günther Prinz, Publizist, ehemaliger Chefredakteur der 'Bild', Deutschland

"Da steht also mein ganzes Leben auf einem Palmenblatt in Madras. Dieses Buch hat mein Verständnis von Raum und Zeit grundlegend verändert."
Fritz Bloomberg, Ex-Vizepräsident Burda Media, New York

"Ein außergewöhnliches Lesevergnügen, das meine Sicht auf die Welt verändert hat."
Gregor Tessnow, Schriftsteller und Drehbuchautor

Breakable - Zerbrechlich

Der Skandalroman aus Mecklenburg

Dieser Psychokrimi hat in der Region, in der es erschien, für so viel Wirbel gesorgt, dass sogar die Presse in die Geschichte eingestiegen ist. Anfeindungen, Intrigen und Klagen finden nicht nur im, sondern fanden auch um das Buch herum statt. Näheres ist einzulesen auf dem Blog

breakablezerbrechlich.wordpress.com

Klappentext:

Eine Frau aus der Stadt. Ein kleines Dorf. Eine alte Köhlerkate, traumhafte Umgebung und idyllische Umgebung. Nicolas Leben könnte nicht friedlicher sein. Eines Tages begegnet sie einem Bauern aus der Nachbarschaft. Es ist Liebe auf den ersten Blick. Als diese von dem Mann mit der unverwechselbaren Stimme auch noch erwidert wird, scheint ihre Welt perfekt.
Doch Nicolas Glück ist nur von kurzer Dauer. Trug und Lüge lauern hinter jeder Ecke. Gerade als sie beginnt, das Ausmaß des Bösen zu entdecken, tun sich Abgründe auf, in die sie niemals hätte schauen dürfen.

Nach einer wahren Begebenheit.

'In ihrem spannenden Roman voller überraschender Volten und psychologischer Abgründe begegnet der Leser Figuren, die er seit Langem zu kennen glaubt.'

Henrik Leschonski, Lektor

Winston

Eine Pferdebuch-Trilogie für Jugendliche

Da Antonia Katharina selbst viele Jahre als Berufsreiterin tätig war, greift sie hier auf einen langjährigen Erfahrungsschatz zurück und veranschaulicht die Welt der Pferde für jeden Leser so realistisch und wirklichkeitsnah, dass man meint, selbst am Geschehen Teil zu nehmen. Ein Pferdeleben, wie es authentischer nicht beschrieben werden kann.

Winston Band I

Ein Fohlen erblickt die Welt

'Da steht er nun. Seine Beine sind viel zu lang für seinen kleinen Körper. Er versucht sich mühsam in der Koordination seiner Bewegungen, die anfangs nur bedingt gelingen. Das Fohlen macht seine ersten Gehversuche und stakst dabei durch das Stroh wie ein Storch durch den Salat.

Es ist wackelig auf den Beinen. Das Neugeborene drückt seinen Körper fest an den seiner Mutter, um stehen zu bleiben und nicht umzukippen. Die Stute bleibt regungslos stehen und wartet, schaut ihr Fohlen an und wagt nicht, sich zu bewegen, sondern bietet mit ihrem großen, ausgewachsenen Körper dem Kleinen Stütze und Orientierung.'

Winston Band II

Die große Show

'Ich wünsche mir aus tiefstem Herzen, dass der Ort, an dem ich bin und alles andere mein Leben lang so bleiben wird wie in diesem Sommer. Das alte Gestüt, in all seiner Stille, entwickelte sich zum unvergesslichen Ort meiner Sehnsucht. Hier will ich sein. Hier gehöre ich her. Und in meinen stillen Augenblicken gibt es nichts, was mir fehlt.

Zwar weiß ich, dass es für die Menschen hier darum geht, Geld zu verdienen, Erfolg zu haben, die Pferde ordentlich auszubilden und teuer zu verkaufen. Doch für mich geht es um den Geruch von frischem Stroh, wenn ich morgens in den Stall komme; um das Glück, das mich durchströmt, wenn ich meine Fohlen auf die Weide lasse; um die Sehnsucht in Winstons Augen, um die warme Sommerluft an lauen Abenden und den unendlichen Frieden, der über den Weiden liegt.

So gingen die Tage ins Land. Alles verlief ruhig. Bis zu jenem Tag, als etwas geschah, was diese Stille durchbrach.'

Winston Band III

Nichts ist unmöglich

'Mein Winston. Niemals hätte ich gedacht, dass man so eine tiefe und innige Beziehung zu einem Pferd haben kann. Dass man sich mit einem Tier so gut verstehen, so klar die Gefühle und Gedanken des anderen erfassen kann; und das alles ohne Worte. Ja, dass man ein Zusammengehörigkeitsgefühl entwickeln kann und eine Nähe, wie das bei uns der Fall ist und das manche Menschen mit allen Worten der Welt niemals herzustellen in der Lage sein werden.'

216